WEST JERUSALEM NOIR

WEST JERUSALEM NOIR

EDITED BY MAAYAN EITAN

TRANSLATED BY YARDENNE GREENSPAN

BROOKLYN, NEW YORK

Published by Akashic Books
©2023 Akashic Books
Copyright to the individual stories is retained by the authors.

Paperback ISBN: 978-1-61775-229-2
Hardcover ISBN: 978-1-63614-168-8
Library of Congress Control Number: 2023933943

Series concept by Tim McLoughlin and Johnny Temple
West Jerusalem map by Sohrab Habibion

Akashic Books
Brooklyn, New York
Instagram, Twitter, Facebook: AkashicBooks
info@akashicbooks.com
www.akashicbooks.com

ALSO IN THE AKASHIC NOIR SERIES

FORTHCOMING

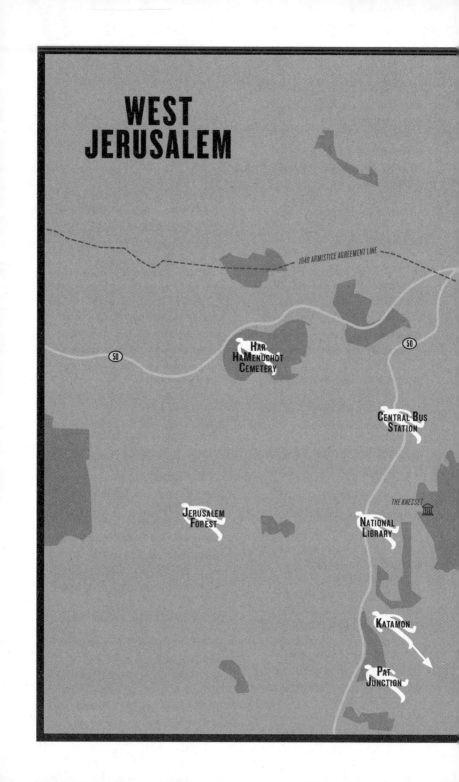

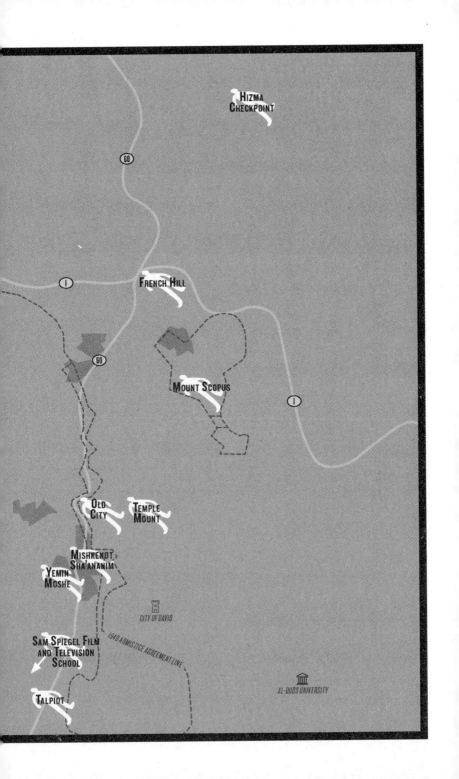

TABLE OF CONTENTS

INTRODUCTION
Nothing More Than Fiction

"**N**o country will more quickly dissipate romantic expectation than Palestine—particularly Jerusalem. To some the disappointment is heartsickening," wrote Herman Melville upon his visit to the city in 1857. Like other Western travelers who came to Jerusalem in the nineteenth century, Melville had trouble reconciling his preconceptions about the city with the reality he discovered. "How it affects one to be cheated in Jerusalem," he added.

Robert Louis Stevenson, Melville's contemporary, reminded us that "sightseeing is the art of disappointment." But to some of Jerusalem's most famous visitors, the disappointment offered by the city seems to have led to utter aggravation. The city never matched their biblical visions; it was scorching hot in summer, dry and chilling in winter; its streets were narrow and dirty, and its people impoverished. The Jerusalem they'd painted in their literary imaginations turned out to be nothing more than fiction.

This anthology offers one more fictional tour of the city, this time through the lens of the noir genre. Not all the stories in this book include a detective, a femme fatale, or a dead body. In fact, a significant number of the writers chose to avoid these genre staples. And yet the stories—each taking place in a different part of the city—sketch a dark imagined map where religious mystery dwells, for example, alongside the quotidian, claustrophobic hubbub of the Central Bus Station.

To kick off *West Jerusalem Noir*, Yiftach Ashkenazi, whose story takes place at a military checkpoint, depicts some of the tragic outcomes of Israeli occupation. Ilana Bernstein chose to place her protagonist within the architectural labyrinth of the Hebrew University's Mount Scopus campus—where she learns that "those who come in here don't leave so quickly," or sometimes at all. Emanuel Yitzchak Levy and Guli Dolev-Hashiloni cowrote a story that offers a new interpretation of the concepts of "Jerusalem Above" and "Jerusalem Below" as they investigate the disappearance of a peccary from the Biblical Zoo. Liat Elkayam's heroine, an occasional detective, is faced with a murder investigation way out of her league.

Asaf Schurr's protagonist finds out just how far a father will go to cover up his daughter's crime, forcing him to relive a traumatic event from his past. In Yardenne Greenspan's story, the Jewish past returns to haunt an old man looking for healing. Ilai Rowner sets two Frenchmen in the largest cemetery in town with a suitcase full of cash to be transferred on behalf of some mysterious "boss." Zohar Elmakias's heroine becomes embroiled in somebody else's story, driving her to visit the Temple Mount over and over, to oblivion.

In Part III, the two detectives in Ilan Rubin Fields's story face the bourgeoisie of the French Hill neighborhood as they search for the arsonist who set a playground on fire. Nano Shabtai presents a coming-of-age story centered around a cruel transition ritual performed in the Jerusalem Forest. Yaara Shehori has written a satire about literature and writers in which war interferes, forcing her protagonist—and us readers—to always remember that Jerusalem is "a city where people could shoot each other in the street."

Tafat Hacohen-Bick and Tehila Hakimi's stories both feature protagonists dealing with disappearances. While

Hacohen-Bick's heroine, whose search leads her into the alleys of the Old City, attempts to find the person closest to her, Hakimi's protagonist, a writer and a new mother, wants to track down a complete stranger she came across at the National Library. Nadav Lapid's main character swings between an omnipotent (though largely imaginary) past to a flawed present in which the death of his and his friends' parents pulls them all back to an unwanted childhood. In the volume's final story, Oded Wolkstein's protagonists are stuck at the Central Bus Station and nearly devoured by the multitude of stimulations this space—not exactly part of the city, but not apart from it either—offers.

The stories included in *West Jerusalem Noir* could not have taken place anywhere else. They reflect national, religious, and socioeconomic tensions inherent to the city and sketch an image of a concrete, contemporary, and complicated Jerusalem. More than a century and a half after Melville's visit, this book offers readers a chance to visit Jerusalem like they've never seen it before.

Maayan Eitan
July 2023

PART I

On That Mountain

A GREAT BUNCH OF GUYS

BY YIFTACH ASHKENAZI

Hizma Checkpoint

Back when we were so young, so green, smelling like the enlistment center, without enough seniority to even do the novice grind, when the most commonly used word in our lives was *bummer*, our company commander made an iron rule: on Fridays, no one could eat before we did a few rounds of fighting songs. He used to be in a support company and believed that the thing that would turn us from no-good novices, from nerdy Nahal people, to infantrymen with poison in our eyes wasn't just runarounds and weekly fuck-up formations, but original fighting songs. So every Friday we sang,

> "Ten, nine, eight, seven
> seven, this is command
> wake up the platoon
> get it together
> we've got a target
> command, this is seven
> wait another hour
> the guys are having fun
> drinking lots of soda
> and oh, the mortars
> oh, the mortars
> they're a great bunch of guys

I wish they weren't such whores . . ."

Or the other, older song:

"I wish the whole brigade
would just drop dead
bulletproof
pack drill
on your back
bullet in the barrel
brother ready for battle . . ."

Two years had gone by since those Fridays on base, during basic training, in a dining hall that smelled like a surface cleaner called Dana, and before I found myself working like a dog in a guard booth on a base physically close to Jerusalem but otherwise very far away. The company commander switched sides and went on a recon tour in a South Lebanon Army car and almost caused a two-sided incident, leading him to be immediately discharged.

We were on a retreat line from Lebanon. The Second Intifada had just started, and we were standing in roadblocks, throwing lockdowns, tossing around riot control measures at quite a few protests, and even going out on a Nahal mission and returning for a final month of service in Jerusalem, which was at that point a target for many terror attacks.

I used to be a total bone during basic training, the kind of guy who was caught with eggshell on his M-16's grip, but I became a MAG operator and a grenade-launch operator, and the company's undisputed combat assigner. Combat assignment, which was not unlike the work done by the Judenrat in the Jewish ghetto, was the job of assigning people to guard duty shifts, and involved lots of conversations in which I tried to prove that I wasn't fucking anyone over or giving anyone special treatment just because I felt like it. It passed the time, and even when people started calling me *Ashke-Nazi* there was a hint of affection in the nickname, which I was in dire need of at the time, just after my father's death. In return, I truly did try to make sure that nobody got screwed over, and when someone had to, I would put myself in that position. That's what happened the morning I went to the front guard post because the only alternative was for the guys who'd just finished a night shift at the checkpoint to go up, and we were short-staffed anyway, meaning they were doing eight-eights—eight hours at the checkpoint and then eight hours' rest, during which the commanders would come up with all sorts of formations or briefings.

After singing the song about Lebanon, where we'd never been, wishing death on the entire brigade, then going into detail (*"I wish all the commanders die / so we don't need the help of officers"*), we also wanted the commanders and the officers to die, if only because they treated us—who would leave the battalion at the end of our training and return to a combat unit after a year of educational activity, as part of the Nahal track—like a track company, and forgot we were all part of the last class, and weren't supposed to endure guard duties and stand around like novices with green berets on our heads and salute. So we did everything we could to handle the dog's life they handed us—instead of being proactive, we played dumb every chance we could. We decided no one would ever go up to guard duty with a beret on, because there was a limit to the shit we were willing to eat. We would never break duty, but that didn't mean we wouldn't show them we'd had enough, we thought, going up to guard duty without berets on. That was our rule. That's what happened when I, Ashke-Nazi, went up to the guard post with Y as part of my job as combat assigner. I did it even though personally I had no problem with the beret. When I'd finished my beret trek I met my parents at the Nahal Memorial and my father was proud. He'd also served in Battalion 50 in the Nahal. Maybe it wasn't the last time he'd been proud of me, but I can't remember any other moment of such clear pride in the year between the beret trek and when he died in a car crash.

Unlike us, Y was a half-jobnik, a boss driver, and didn't toil like the rest of us, which caused many to claim that he wasn't a fighter like us but part of headquarters, just like the female social services soldiers, who everyone wanted to fuck and who some claimed to have. Now that he was just a simple soldier like everybody else, Y started to act all high and mighty and pretend to be super motivated. If he had just acted like a motivated poser, no one would have made a fuss. But when he started playing like he was Rambo with the Palestinians at the Qalandia checkpoint, acting like Abu Antar putting taxi drivers in his sights and yelling at them, "Where's your tasrih? Where's your papers?" some people got riled up. The warning he got soon became realized through graffiti sprayed on every hitchhiking shelter in the area: *Y is an enlightened occupier.*

Y couldn't care less about the graffiti. He didn't give a shit. The thing that got his panties in a twist during that guard shift were the two medics who suddenly decided to grow a conscience and announced they wouldn't be grinding at the checkpoint like everyone else. At most they would be war-room runners, waking up the new shifts and then going back to sitting on their asses. Y tried to convince me it was just an act: "It's not that they hate standing at the checkpoint with us, they just want to screw us over, and you're playing into their hands when you let them get away with it. You're letting them fuck us over, Ashke-Nazi, don't you get it?"

When that didn't work, he started singing fighting songs, trying to prove to me and to himself that he was a mega-fighter, a real infantryman, and that the rest of us were just losers. He didn't stop at the death of the brigade and the death of commanders and officers, but kept going until the final verse, the one that follows the death of the soldier in Lebanon:

> "Now I'm an angel
> an angel among angels
> taking hits off the bong
> marijuana
> mint and verbena
> and high-high-high all day long . . ."

It was precisely because our boot camp company commander had made sure we knew the fighting songs by heart and could recite the words even if someone woke us up in the middle of the night, precisely because I knew every word, that I was able to tune Y out and instead think about myself. I'd chosen to go into a Nahal unit, just like my father, but when the time came, I wasn't so sure. My father had fought in the Six-Day War and the Yom Kippur War and the First Lebanon War, and I thought I might let him down if I only spent two years in the infantry rather than three. Ultimately, when I decided not to leave the seed and spent a year away from combat duty, he died, and then I regretted my choice, sad to think I might have disappointed him. That same sorrow caused me, after he died, to obsess about having a Leatherman pocketknife, something that would make me feel like a resourceful warrior, and so I convinced my mother, who was still reeling, to buy me one. It wasn't so much the money she spent that upsets me now, it was how I kept talking her ear off about a pocketknife like some idiot kid, shitting all over everything she was going through.

My shame for that moment of helplessness—exacerbated by the heat of the ugly yellow desert that wrapped around Jerusalem from the east, and the burnt smell rising from Khan al-Ahmar, which was defined as a hostile village with terrorist warnings even though it just looked like a sad, impoverished little place—was cut short when a sketchy-looking Subaru with Palestinian license plates came at us at full speed.

Y cocked his rifle to start a suspect arrest procedure, but luckily he was too much of a bone to finish it before the car pulled up, and out came a father carrying a four- or five-year-old kid with a sea of blood pouring from his head. He wasn't a terrorist—he was a father whose son had gotten hit by a car and now he was coming to us for help. We reported the incident over the radio and one of the medics Y had accused of being lazy sprinted over right away and tried to resuscitate the kid. Finally, he determined that only a medevac could save him.

I got hold of the brigade over the radio and asked them to send a chopper, but they wanted to know if the kid was Israeli or a local. When I told them he was a local, they asked, "Was it our doing?" When I told them it wasn't, they said there was no approval to send a chopper. This kid was never going to get a chopper and would be better off gunning it to the hospital in Ramallah. The man banged his fist against the hood of the Subaru and cried. Maybe even a medevac wouldn't have helped. He drove slowly in reverse with the dead kid in his car, and we stayed behind with the puddle of blood that was later removed with Dana surface cleaner, whose infamous smell was familiar to us from boot camp, just like the word *bummer*, which Y used to summarize the event. I agreed.

If Y started singing "I Wish the Whole Brigade Would Die" just then, I would have joined him with poison in my eyes, just like those Fridays during basic training with the company commander who came from the support company, condemning the brigade that had prevented Y and me from being truly enlightened occupiers, a source of pride. I wasn't that green anymore, no longer just a novice who smelled like the enlistment center, but I was green enough not to admit to myself that my father would never be proud of me again, that even the sorrow of writing is a result of the fact that I can't manage to be a writer whose work is a source of pride. Writers don't have the extenuating circumstances that the fighting song gave the mortars. The whorish nature of writing, the one that allows a writer to write about a dead father, about a child dying in his father's arms, to really write only about himself, does not allow the same writer to tell himself he's a great guy; he only feels sorrow and regret.

YOU CAN'T SEE THE OCCUPATION FROM HERE

BY ILANA BERNSTEIN

Mount Scopus

L ate at night, on the last bus, on my way to work, I delved into a shooting incident broadcasted on a loop on one of the news websites. In the video taken by an eyewitness, a cleaning woman was seen in the final moments of her life. The shooting, it was reported, was an act of terrorism. The location wasn't mentioned, but I could easily identify the looping hallway at the Mount Scopus campus, near one of the cafeterias.

I myself work in Mount Scopus in a sort of lab. A communications lab. Not that we study communications there, at least not the kind that would naturally come to mind. At any rate, it isn't a university-run research lab, but one sponsored by the university. Something like that. Some people claim it doesn't exist at all. Others tell a story about some experimental project that had been shut down due to a lack of funding. No one volunteers many details. Everything is offered with curious stinginess. Some people claim that ultimately, after switching quite a few hands, the questionable study of pheromones was brought back to the university and got somehow stuck here on the mountain, in the Humanities Department, of all places.

People talk about a collaboration between the university and—well, that's the thing, no one knows who the university is collaborating with. It's easy to offer conjectures, but there is no proof. Either way, certain things will be realized later or become even more complicated than they already are. This is a rolling process making its way through the campus circuit.

I played the video again, hoping to glean more details. My bones shivered at the horrible sights. My pulse quickened. My blood rushed from the soles of my feet to the roots of my hair. My breathing grew heavy. No one on the bus seemed to notice. A few passengers were self-absorbed, their eyes glassy. Others' chins pecked the middle of their collarbones; they dozed off and then sat up and repeated the action. I didn't recognize the security officer. I wondered if he was the shooter or if the shooter had already taken off by that point. But it was easy to recognize the murdered cleaning lady. She worked in our lab, and one of my colleagues liked to call her "the CEO."

I'm new at the lab, filling in for the regular translator, who's on maternity leave. I'm grateful for my good fortune. Few people get these positions, perhaps because few people have the necessary sense of direction. To make it in this academic maze, on its many branching corridors, seen and hidden spaces, attics and cellars, and—some claim—catacombs (not the Cave of Nicanor on the north part of campus, but fresh graves dug in the unmarked, invisible spaces between walls), one must also possess more than just spatial orientation.

Composure, for one. Because it's so easy to get lost here, and we are forbidden from asking for help or looking around. We are also not allowed to turn back, no matter what. We must blend into the space, avoid standing out in any way, even at the price of endless circling. But true loitering is against the rules. It's best not to show helplessness when one loses their way or turns in the wrong direction, to prevent a situation in which anyone, god forbid, offers their assistance. Though this isn't typically a danger. The people around us are not ones to rush to help others. Mutual aid is not part of the culture of this place.

We are also not permitted to answer the calls of students, lecturers, or administration workers, and certainly not any questions from the security guards flooding the campus, soldiers in uniforms, or other innocent bystanders who are always suspected of being undercover agents, sometimes even from our side. You can never know.

Naturally, things are ten times more complicated during the day when the campus labyrinth is visited by international tourists who repeatedly find themselves at the forum instead of the synagogue, asking for help over and over again. The lab, in case I haven't already mentioned it, is active at all hours of the day and night. We have to pretend we either don't hear them or don't understand them, then disappear into one of the rooms, the faculty offices or bathroom. We can also seek refuge in the abandoned computer lab, in the adjacent workspaces, or near the abandoned photocopier stations. It doesn't matter, as long as we keep moving.

Working here involves quite a few sacrifices. We sacrifice our privacy, connection with the outside world, and stability. Working here requires tolerance of closed, stifled spaces, self-control, and a readiness to abandon one's desk at a moment's notice.

The people who survive at this job are the kind who suffer from agoraphobia and prefer sealed-off rooms to daylight and natural air. People of contradictions: on the one hand, dominant and aggressive; on the other, anxious folks who rely on the observation tower overlooking the Judean Desert, as well as us. I didn't believe I possessed all the necessary qualities, but my colleague proved me wrong. I wouldn't have been hired had I not fit the bill.

I don't have much to say about the work itself. It's a job like any other. In fact, I'm forbidden from talking about it. I've been working here for three weeks and yet I still don't know what we're studying or developing. We have no access to the lab itself. Its physical existence is out of sight, and there's no point in asking. No one will disclose the tiniest crumb of information. There is a level of secrecy to everything, of course. I agreed to this when I signed the contract. I endeavor to maintain confidentiality, and not just during my period of employment, but for seven years after completing my contract. Long after I'll have stopped working here. And yet.

Don't be so sure, my colleague says. Those who come in here don't leave so quickly. Unless we make a mistake, we'll be growing old here. By their terms—the terms of the company that hired me—that which is temporary is permanent. Our titles change. Roles are constantly switched. I've worked as a typist for three days. I've even spent some time in maintenance. This happened after only five days on the job. The managers brought up the possibility of role-switching due to security sensitivity. Obviously I wasn't offered a department management job. And I can assure you, you'll never find a manager at the typist's desk or carrying a screwdriver. No complaints are allowed. I've signed a contract.

It's the kind of contract you can't remove from the office or send to a lawyer, which my husband just happens to be. I memorized quite a few clauses that seemed draconian, though by the time I got back home I could no longer remember them. It's because of the hormones, my colleague said. I gave birth three months ago. But she had other suspicions. It sounds similar, she said, but these people study pheromones, not hormones. I didn't see her again after we had this exchange. These people are so sensitive.

Whatever the case, I don't understand what all these signatures are for. I know nothing of the nature of the research being conducted here anyway. Try as they might, no one would be able to extort me. I've got nothing to give. No information to share. I don't even know how many people work here or what their official titles are. Everybody is temporary or defined as temporary. Everyone but senior management, of course. At least I think so. At any rate, I can't tell a junior manager from a senior manager. Many do disappear, then pop up again in other offices, on other days, sometimes months later, or so my colleague claims. People whom everyone was convinced were gone from this world, either naturally or through some expedited procedure.

I assume they have offices on other campuses too, not only Hebrew University campuses. With each passing day, we fathom the power of the organization we work for. The company. The lab or this thing posing as a lab, whose records we keep and whose studies we translate. The lab that none of us have access to, but which pays our salaries through the data it collects and the impressive results it yields. For some reason, strangers know more about where I work than I do. Or at least they think they know. You work for the hush-hush industry, they say, chuckling. They all realize that the university is a dignified cloak. Either way, going by this logic, I'll be finding myself at a different office one of these days, possibly even with a different husband and a baby who isn't mine. That's an interesting premise.

In the meantime, I send files from here to there and vice versa. But where's here and where's there? I don't know. I

translate bits of text, partial documents, intentionally frag-
mented. Sometimes I recognize their continuation in papers
in other languages I am given to translate. The only ones
who see the big picture are our superiors, who aren't at the
office. For all I know, the head of the Student Association
could be one of them, or the classics professor. Someone once
suggested that the president of the university was involved.
Rumors circulate ceaselessly. But in spite of everything, I refuse to believe that the president of the university has any job
beyond his official capacity.

My colleague—that is, my changing colleague—told me
that a woman runs the company, a female CEO. And if this
news alone wasn't astounding enough, she added: a Palestinian woman. My colleague had lost all touch with reality. I'm
too afraid to mention it out loud, but it's getting dangerous
now. It's getting to the point where I'm going to have to report her. When this CEO comes to visit, my colleague also
says, she wears the institutional powder-blue coat of sanitary
workers, her head covered with a floral pink and cerulean
hijab.

What about national security? I asked. She answered
quickly, as if her response had been dictated in advance, prepared in her mouth for these very scenarios. As if nothing is
random. Everything intended to avoid any suspicions that
we are a security industry facility, or one conducting research
and development for the security industry. Security is said to
be nothing but a euphemism. We are guests of the university,
holding conferences and symposiums and pop-up research
labs. That's the information I have, anyway. The CEO even
cleans the place by herself, my colleague said. You've surely
seen her.

I continued listening intently, since, as everyone knows,

if there is truth, it is often concealed behind lies, though I had trouble camouflaging my smile. That's how it goes—in the absence of organized information, the mind wanders and the mushrooms of conspiracy pop up everywhere.

Remember the cleaner who came here last week? The one who gathered the paper flakes from the shredders? my colleague asked.

I remember, I said. She had a headscarf with a print of cherry blossoms on a backdrop of blue skies.

That's her. We have to recognize the workers, and whenever a new face appears, which happens almost daily, we must report it through the proper channels.

But we burn the documents, we have office incinerators, I said. Then I pointed at my own personal incinerator, positioned next to my desk. What paper flakes are you talking about?

My colleague raised her chin, implying that she could say no more on the matter. She raised her eyebrows in a matching gesture.

From that day on, I started tracking—with my eyes only—the changing cleaners. I searched their eyes for the one who could be the head of the company. Not only their eyes. I looked them over, head to toe, seeking clues in their jewelry, if they wore any, in the quality of their footwear, in the locks of hair that slipped out of their head coverings. The ones who wore headscarves actually looked Jewish to me, while the bare-headed ones appeared Palestinian. My colleague explained that there was a difference in the type of headscarves the women of different faiths wore, but I had trouble telling the difference. One cleaner's headscarf stood out, unique. If my colleague was right, and our CEO is a woman, she is likely a Jew posing as a Palestinian posing as a

Jew. From that moment on, I searched for a sanitary worker who met this description.

Forget the contract, I told my husband, but the number of riders I had to sign was beyond imaginable. I didn't tell him about the medical forms I had to fill out, the psycho-didactic or psycho-whatever testing, some kind of personality testing. Of course I was prohibited from describing the many tests I had to pass in order to be hired by this company, which was desirable mostly because of the high pay, since it was impossible to brag about the product. Rumors of job openings are passed through word of mouth. I also couldn't talk about the unending multiple-choice quizzes, the final few of which, I can attest, were intended only to trick us. No matter how hard you work your brain, you cannot come up with the correct answer. It's like the paradoxes about red traffic lights and Epimenides's "all Cretans are liars."

But in all honesty, I'm better off keeping quiet anyway. I probably shouldn't offer any details. People might think I've lost my mind. In this place, any preliminary warning signs point you to the exit, which is not the doorway to freedom, as one might assume. I often think I'm on my way there now— on my way to insanity, that is. But people around me reassure me, promising me that everyone feels this way at first, that I'm a fast learner, and that my superiors are satisfied with my adjustment.

And all this effort is made just to get a temporary position, which my colleague promised is not as temporary as it may seem, assuming I don't break the rules. It's financially rewarding, anyway. That is the answer to the question *Why work here, under these nutty conditions?* which I pose to myself from time to time.

I know by heart the script I received upon signing my

contract. Maybe some of you can read between the lines and figure this out, but I can't. It's a short piece of writing, just a few words that I can conjure whenever anyone asks me where I work, what I do for a living, and what positions my superiors hold. I was made to memorize it in their presence, and it wasn't as easy as it might seem. The whole situation was embarrassing. I tried a couple of times, but couldn't get through the second sentence. We're patient people, they said. They chorused it. A two-person chorus. My direct superior and the office manager. This often happens to them. They know each other better than a married couple. If it wasn't for their incongruent looks, I would never be able to guess which one was addressing me. Indeed, they had patience. Iron patience. They must have been rooting for me because of my knowledge of languages. I speak, read, and write five languages. They even ignored the fact that I'd just had a baby. I told them it was a plus—being postpartum, there was no way I would be going on maternity leave anytime soon. I was insinuating my strength over the employee I was replacing. One must step over bodies if one wishes to get ahead.

Babies are not welcome here, mostly because mothers must often miss work when their children are sick, etc. It is no accident that at the top of the daily questionnaire—about which I can't say much, except that it contains twenty-one questions that have nothing obvious to do with each other, no unequivocal answers, or answers at all—we must state how much time we've invested in our home life and families on the previous workday, and how emotionally involved we are with our domestic existence in comparison to the workplace. These people have measurement methods too complex to discuss here. We very well may be part of their research.

The office I work for deals with the research and development of communications. That's how my memorized script begins. Then they wanted me to say: *Our goal is* . . . But I told them that nobody actually talks that way. It would be better if I said, *What we do is* . . . And they agreed, even though I've been told time and time again that this is not the place to show initiative. The office I work for wants a lack of initiative, and that suits me fine. A lack of initiative but an excess of efficiency. We like to think outside the box, the managers said, and there's no one left who will think inside the box. That's what I was hired to do, and I've been deep inside the box ever since. All I see is walls. From the inside, of course. At this stage in my life, no atmosphere is better suited to me than the inside of a box. The last thing I want is a job where I have to invent myself, or worse, take my work home with me. All I want is to do good work during working hours, and walk out of the office at the end of the day knowing I can leave everything behind and use my spare time to take care of my baby. Take care of him and play with him. He likes to play, even though he is only three months old. I'm preparing for this kind of trick question in the daily questionnaire. A question about babies' playing habits or the patience exhibited by tired young mothers moving between home and work.

Well then, the office I work for deals with the research and development of communication, from the idea stage to planning and mathematical modeling. This is where we stop. We make nothing. What we do is allow anyone to send huge files—audio and video—fast and in high quality. My husband told me dozens of other companies are already working on this project. Already making it happen. It's essentially an existing product, he explained. They're fooling you. They don't want you to know what they're really doing.

And I *don't* know, I told him. Of course it's a cover-up.

I didn't even know what he was trying to say. I knew from the start that this wasn't about communications the way we understand it. It was clear when I saw pheromones appearing in several documents, including the first one I translated as part of my entry exams. This is about advanced regressive communication.

My husband laughed. You're talking in oxymorons, he said.

You got us, I said. That's exactly what we research and develop.

As you may have gathered, I'm a young mother. This is my first job since having my child, and it's no coincidence that I'm replacing a woman who has gone on maternity leave. At this point, after a few weeks at the job, I wouldn't be surprised to find that this place requires the inspiration of pregnancy and postpartum hormones. It's no coincidence that the word *pheromone* is made up of the words *phero*—meaning *to bear*— and *hormone*. The office manager even implied as much when he said, One just before birth and the other just after birth, it's been this way for years.

But that isn't the only factor in me being offered the job. They need a feminine point of view. Or a female point of view, anyway. A woman's mind, pregnant or not. Or, ideally, a pregnancy that does not culminate with a child. I admit I agreed to undergo periodic blood and urine testing, and to ask no questions, and yet it's hard for me to ignore the fact that all the managers are men, and all the lower-ranking employees are women, perhaps due to the synchronizing of women's cycles as a result of pheromone discharge—a conjecture that has yet to be founded. On second thought, that might not be right. Certain types of female mice synchronize cycles due to the pheromones of a male mouse in the area. All of this information was dropped on me during the translation work. Either way, there are outliers that prove the rule. I wasn't sure about that last sentence. My husband nodded his default nod. Perhaps he is part of the company too, and his questioning was intended to test me. Or perhaps he is the discharging male. Or the dissipater. I'm not sure which title is more appropriate.

My direct supervisor has told me on more than one occasion that the employee demographics are a coincidence. Young women, who are the majority of our workforce, are also women statistically placed in the childbearing years of their lives. They get their periods with awe-inspiring regularity, and their ability to synchronize with their colleagues is even more astonishing. I knew I shouldn't press or ponder the topic too much. What could I possibly discover? That we are a weak link? That our physical and mental states are fragile? I'd reached these conclusions long ago, without sniffing around.

Obviously, confidentiality dictates that our offices change locations regularly, and no site is better for hiding one's tracks than the Mount Scopus campus. A university that is a virtual fortress. Instead of windows we have embrasures. You can't see the occupation from here, I told my colleague, who is also revolving, as you may have gathered. Or perhaps I am the revolving one. It's intentional, I added before she could shush me. If the students could see where they are, they'd start asking questions.

Even though we were whispering, my supervisor overheard us. The managers around here must clean their ears diligently. There is no other explanation for the prevalence of used Q-tips in the trash cans.

You don't understand anything, he said. This campus echoes the walls of the Old City. There is architectural thought behind this. And interwall communication, I added silently. The al-Aqsa Mosque on one side, he said, and our synagogue just across the way. I thought about how the synagogue was swallowed into the structure and might not even be situated across from the mosque, but I chose not to share this opinion. He said nothing about the Dome of the Rock, but I caught his drift. I figured it all out. The Hebrew University's Mount Scopus campus is our answer to the Dome of the Rock. An architectural menace in response to an architectural marvel. Space-occupying architecture. I knew I should keep my mouth shut. I would find no fans here, regardless of which part of my thoughts I expressed.

Sometimes we have to switch offices in the middle of a workday. In a single moment, everything is packed up in boxes, leaving no trace. That's also why we are forbidden from bringing any personal belongings into the office. I can't even keep a framed picture of my child on my desk. Instead, I carry it in my bag and glance at it during smoke breaks. But most of the time we know when a move is coming up, since we are the ones who send the coded files to everybody in the office. At this rate, there won't be an office, a basement, or a classroom we won't occupy for a bit.

From the outside, we look just like any other campus office, no matter which room we use. Exhausted employees staring at computer screens in badly lit, stuffy rooms. Sometimes our entire company has to squeeze into a single classroom. When this happens, an outsider might think we're in the middle of a conference. Three of us sit at a wide desk in front of a whiteboard. One stands at the podium. The rest are scattered on the seats intended for students. Apart from the big lecture hall where I took my entry exams, I like the small humanities classrooms on the bottom floor. From the windows, I can see fragments of the view. I say fragments since from most of these rooms, the view, already limited by the narrow windows, is blocked by the basement roof, which is also fenced in.

Yesterday, following an alert sent to the managers, we vacated the machine room and set up shop in room 6837. A lecture hall. Since the school year is over, we can expect to stay here awhile. We all love this room where, as I mentioned, I underwent my entry exams. We love it not because of its beauty. Acute angles, steep slopes, cheap-looking seats, and the intimidating maw of the seemingly Roman semicircular orchestra are no testament to fine taste. We like it because it's wood-paneled, spacious, too big for us, really. We love it because of the piano—we often pretend to be rehearsing for a musical interlude at a future conference. Most of all, we love it because it feels as if at any moment the lights might go out and a movie will start. Of course, that never happens. I don't think it's even possible to screen movies in this room. But it's certainly possible to play music. In fact, there was even room for a second piano.

My colleague and I situated ourselves on the right-hand staircase overlooking the stage, in the back row, just by one of the exits. As soon as we sat down, the cleaner walked in. The CEO, to take my colleague's word for it. She was carrying a bucket containing a rag and a wood-cleaning spray.

What time is it? I asked her.

The cleaner didn't answer.

Maybe she doesn't speak Hebrew, I suggested. Or maybe she's hard of hearing.

But my colleague interpreted her ignoring me as proof positive of her being the CEO of the company. You see? she said. She didn't even answer you.

We picked up our laptops to allow her to wipe down the

desks, but the cleaner chose to descend to the orchestra and clean the piano, of all things. She's a cleaner who can't clean, said my colleague. Now do you believe me?

My direct supervisor approached her and said something we couldn't hear. That was another sign. What reason did he have to speak to the cleaner? But I wasn't convinced. All I could see was a cleaner, most likely a contract worker, a woman with a hunched back and an expressionless face. A woman whose institutional powder-blue coat was too big for her frame, hiding a dress worn over pants. Maybe she's a settler, a familiar thought crossed my mind. Is this the woman I've been looking for?

She really is deaf, I told my colleague. She's using sign language.

She's just gesticulating, said my colleague. Lots of people do that.

Sometimes I wonder if there are other companies of our kind—a kind I am not at liberty to define here or elsewhere—working on campuses under the cloak of secrecy. Logic has it that if there is one, there must be others. There are military personnel everywhere, as if they are in the middle of a maneuver. Command center drills, deploying and evacuating a field camp, using two-way radios, camouflage, and security, including information systems security. All very similar to what we do. But for us this is neither a drill nor a military operation. We are an allegedly civilian company, even though many of our employees used to serve in the military's most elite units. Either way, ever since the university opened its gates to soldier-students, in addition to the armed reserve duty soldiers who had already been wandering these parts, the campus has felt more like an enormous base. Is the Hebrew University transforming into a military academy?

I wouldn't be surprised if she served in Unit 6200, I told my colleague.

I served in Unit 7200, my colleague offered without a second thought. I mean, I could have served there, she corrected, panicking. Well, actually, I guess that isn't a secret. You must have served there too, no?

The cleaner wiped off every wooden surface, the desks' sides flush against the chairs like rulers. Apart from her brief exchange with my supervisor, she did nothing but clean. My own arm hurt just from following her beautiful curving motions. Three hours went by from the moment she walked into the lecture hall until the moment she left.

The next day, I stopped at the student cafeteria, the only one still open at this hour, and bought a cheddar sandwich left over from the morning, a strong latte, and a water. It was seven minutes to midnight, and I decided to sit down at one of the tables so I could eat uninterrupted. I recalled the question from the previous day's questionnaire: How many grains of sand are the minimum to make a pile: 500, 1,000, 1,500, or none of the above? I couldn't make a guess.

I looked around. The campus was deserted, darkness filling the hallways. The cafeteria, so crowded during finals, was now empty. I noticed that the barista and the cashier were chatting in Arabic. Or, rather, the barista was speaking Arabic and the cashier was mumbling unintelligibly. He told her to speak up and enunciate, but she continued to mumble. Her speech was like one long, meandering, meaningless word. I turned my head to hear better. I couldn't get that CEO out of my mind. When I looked again, she was standing behind the cash register instead of the cashier who had charged me just a few minutes earlier. It was the woman my colleague claims is the CEO. And not just a woman, but a Palestinian woman. She was the one who'd been mumbling. She was using hand gestures again.

Without planning to, I got up to buy a chocolate bar so I could speak to her without appearing rude. I wanted to get to the bottom of this. I stood across from her, chocolate bar in hand, waiting for her to name the price, as was customary. But the cashier said nothing. We stood like this for a long moment. I was holding my purse, but was in no rush to pull out my credit card. Like a gun duel, we each waited for the other one to draw. My body emitted distress pheromones. Fear, even.

I broke first. As soon as I put the chocolate bar down on the counter, the barista walked over and pushed the woman. She stumbled, then steadied herself.

What are you doing? I said.

The cleaner started to cry. Her hands were explaining something I couldn't understand.

I turned around, grabbed my bag from my table, and left, heading to room 6837.

It was so quiet that night that I could hear my footsteps. But soon, I heard more than that. Another pair of feet was walking behind me, and another pair behind that. I knew I shouldn't turn around, especially if I was being followed. I kept my cool, as is expected of us. I tried to recreate the final image in my mind: was anyone else there besides the cleaner and the barista?

Stop or I'll shoot, an authoritative male voice said. I stopped. Stop or I'll shoot, the voice that suddenly reminded me of the security guard repeated. The guard who stood right by the escalator at the underground bus station. Even though I stopped, I heard a gunshot behind me, followed by a thump.

A human body collapsing onto the floor. A body that was not my own. The head of the company. The CEO. The cleaner. The Palestinian. The cashier. The mumbler. My colleague. You can go, the voice said. Like a windup toy, I started on my way again.

I spent my morning break immersed in a shooting incident broadcasted on a loop on one of the news websites. In the video taken by an eyewitness, a cleaning woman was seen in the final moments of her life. The shooting, it was reported, was an act of terrorism. The woman, an Arab citizen from one of the East Jerusalem neighborhoods, was forty-one at the time of her death, and left behind a husband and two children.

I heard the gunshot, I told my colleague. And the thump.

Did you turn around to look? she asked.

We're not allowed to turn around, I told her. You know that.

DOS IS NISHT A KHAZIR

BY EMANUEL YITZCHAK LEVI AND GULI DOLEV-HASHILONI

Katamon

The Moon Grove was filled with grassless clearings, as empty as the stone path on its outskirts. Shmulik paced ravenous circles, trying in vain to bite his own tail. His desperate eyes turned to the sky, but he found it just beginning to brighten and knew he had to wait at least another hour before breakfast. This strange boy he'd been charged with tossed over a pink tennis ball from the bushes, but Shmulik didn't want to play. He'd long ago tired of the idle life, and longed for the regular meals at the zoo. But he had no idea how to get back home. Nevertheless, the instant he felt a tremble in his foot, he forgot all about his yearnings. He jumped backward, watching the expanding gap between the paving stones, until the familiar boy rose carefully from the small hole that had opened up, wearing a striped dress and carrying a bucket. Shmulik sniffed the dirt on the boy's knees and licked his shin. Wasting no time, the boy pulled juicy apples from his pockets and offered them to Shmulik. And as the excited piglet gobbled up the feast, the boy bent down and pushed the two stones back together. Unable to fully close the gap, he patched it up with plaster from the bucket in his hand.

By the time Be'eri woke up on the living room couch, the Shabbat candles were already burning. Looking around, he found that though his uncle and cousins had already left, the sun was still visible in the sky. He quickly grabbed his laptop, taking advantage of that precious period between the lighting of the candles and the setting of the sun. The letters he'd doodled onto a grocery store receipt, bloating and growing cumbersome as slumber threatened to take over, he now copied into his email draft with hasty keyboard taps, mixing up his *i*'s and *u*'s.

Before he'd taken off for his sabbatical at Princeton University, Dr. Atad Nahumi, Be'eri's father, had agreed to leave him in his aunt and uncle's care, as long as Be'eri read a Torah portion at synagogue every Friday afternoon after he'd sent the portion to Atad's university email address before the Shabbat started. "And that's another fatal mistake that will send me to the cardiologist," Be'eri had heard Atad telling his wife the night before they left the country, "abandoning this nebbish boy to the influence of your meshuga brother. He will probably take him to his egalitarian minyan, to pick up young divorcées." Once again, his father brought up Rabbi Mario's days as a young Trotskyite in Padua, promoting "Halacha-approved" free love and writing for local "papers," until, at age thirty-eight, he found himself jobless and wifeless and decided to become a neo-orthodox rabbi in Jerusalem. "Because, if you are already not working, why not get paid for it?" Atad concluded with deep disdain, pouring himself diluted buttermilk from the clear jug that always, always waited for him in the refrigerator door.

Be'eri emailed the Torah portion and was filled with bitterness when he realized there were only five minutes left before sunset. He turned off his phone, rushed to take a one-minute lukewarm shower, put on his Shabbat best, and walked out with his grocery store receipt toward the egalitarian synagogue on Elazar HaModa'i Street. The neighborhood was tumultuous, just like every Friday night, but this time not because of the humming of Carlebach's, the bouncing of basketballs, or the murmurings of little girls at the empty bus stops, unashamed to stare at every passerby. Rather, it came from the gangs of boys who scampered through the streets, crying, "Shmulik! Shmulik!" as they bent down to look under benches and overturned trash cans. That morning, Mario showed Be'eri the piece on the *Voice of Town* website, reporting that Shmulik the peccary had escaped from his cage in the Biblical Zoo. Someone must not have closed the back gate, the one overlooking Refaim Stream, and now the zoo was offering a bounty on the head of the fugitive—an annual zoo membership and a stuffed rhino.

Now Be'eri, walking quickly but ponderously, paying no mind to anything taking place outside of his own head, recalled the day he'd first seen the peccary at the zoo. He'd loved the zoo as an eight-year-old—he'd spent hours reading a nature encyclopedia, memorizing the animals' Latin names and their ages of sexual maturation, staring at the corpses of cats on the sides of the roads and wondering whether their lives could have been saved. Although his father hated animals, and the burning sun, and the zoo architect who'd built roads going uphill only, and Be'eri's mother who just had to hang around that day with her doltish friends, and the giraffe—because what the hell was a giraffe doing at the Biblical Zoo, giraffes are not mentioned even in the Ethiopian *Book of Enoch*—and Professor Pitussi, who was sabotaging his tenure; so by the time they reached the peccary cage, he was already livid.

The peccary was a South American mammal, and Be'eri remembered that, though it resembled a pig, it categorically was not a pig. But after some hidden righteous ones hurled stones at the impure beast, the zoo manager added a formal sign to the gate, reading, *The Peccary Is Not a Pig*, and added a Yiddish translation: *Dos Is Nisht a Khazir*. As far as Atad was concerned, that sign was the straw that broke the camel's back. He pounded his fist against it repeatedly. The herd of peccaries, big and small, panicked and ran to and fro in their cage.

A zoo employee shouted at Atad, "What are you doing, you moron?"

Atad walked over quickly and tried to grab the man's collar. "You damn heathens! So educated and enlightened in your own eyes, telling us the difference between a hog and a dog!" he roared. "But the Bible you have learned not, and of proper Yiddish you have not heard!"

He started pounding the sign again, before the eyes of the stunned zoo visitors, yelling, "*Dos is nisht* keyn *Khazir! Dos is nisht* keyn *Khazir!!*" until the zoo employee fled and returned with a security guard. Atad and Be'eri were banned from entering the zoo for the rest of their lives.

Now Be'eri arrived at entrance of the tiny synagogue, hidden in the back of the yard. He heard the sonorous voice of his Aunt Gisella leading the Shabbat prayer, and realized that it was a matter of minutes before his uncle would summon him to recite the Torah portion, and once again his knees would buckle and his tongue would falter. His stomach flooded with a warm fog of desperation and he dropped himself onto a nearby bench. Suddenly, he noticed that the shadow cast over him had not come from the heavens, but from an awkward girl who had stepped out of the synagogue and was glaring at him. Her dirty shorts and tank top told him she'd ended up at the synagogue by mistake.

"Excuse me," Be'eri said, "need any help?"

"Do you belong to this synagogue?" she asked.

He didn't dare look directly at her, trying instead to envision her features by the tone of her voice. She had an unidentifiable accent, something between German and Hungarian. "Yes," he said, "my uncle is the rabbi. Is something wrong?"

"No, just ended up here. I'm Araunah."

"Good," said Be'eri, who didn't quite know how to reply. He lowered his eyes to the cracks between the sidewalk stones. The stones were set crisscross, and the one the girl stood on in her sandals was the only stone attached to its neighbor without any gap. She continued to stare at him, so he asked, "Are you all set for tonight? Do you have a place to eat?"

"Nope."

"Want me to ask my uncle?" Be'eri was glad for an excuse to slip away from her. "He'll probably know. There must be a family here who would be happy to have you over—"

"How 'bout you?" the girl interrupted, rolling herself a cigarette. "What are you up to tonight?"

"I'm having dinner with my aunt and uncle."

"Wanna go to a bar with me?"

"Tonight . . . I don't think a bar is a good idea."

At last, he dared to look directly at her. Her head was narrow, her fair hair shorn, making her ears protrude. Her lips were thick and soft, her body barely clad in short-shorts and a plain tank top, braless. He wondered what kind of an odd bird would invite a boy wearing a yarmulke to a bar on a Friday night. Maybe a tourist. Yet her Hebrew was good.

At that moment, his aunt fell silent and somebody said the Kaddish prayer. Then Rabbi Mario came over to the doorway and signaled for Be'eri, who nodded and walked inside, the girl following suit. Inside the synagogue, his little cousin took his arm and led him to the stage. Mario's shtibl was enormous, and everybody stared at him from both the women's and men's sides: his uncles and cousins and IDF colonels and female rabbis and his father's boss, Professor Pitussi, everyone in Shabbat clothes, and off to the side was this stranger in her ugly tank top, extinguished cigarette in her hand, for which no one dared admonish her. Be'eri coughed and glanced at the paper he was holding, then back at the girl, then at the paper, until he grew dizzy, and started reading his sermon off the receipt without looking at anyone.

"So in this week's Torah portion, the Lord demands that when the Israelites come to the Land of Israel, they shall not create an alliance with the original dwellers of this land, and not enter marriages with them." Be'eri looked at the girl, who was smiling at him from the last bench, drinking up his every word.

"And this is where we come across an issue of interpretation, because in the Book of Exodus, God promises Moses He will expel all the other peoples living in the Land of Canaan. *The Amorite, the Canaanite, the Hittite, the Perizzite, the Hivite, and the Jebusite.*" Be'eri hated himself deeply as he began to stutter, hanging on Araunah's eyes. For he realized that to her, he now represented something racist, monstrous, prehistoric. He knew he was hurting her, humiliating her.

"But if the Lord banishes the Jebusites, how could there still be a chance of them tempting us to marriage?" he asked, his voice trembling.

All of a sudden, he feared that his caution would render him misunderstood. He buried his face in the receipt and searched for an improvisational path, unable to decipher a single useful line among the tightly lettered text. "So, do you get the problem? I mean . . . you see—" yet terror paralyzed him. He lifted his head up, saw that the girl was gone, then lowered his head in silence. His knees trembled. He looked up a few times as if preparing to continue, but remained silent. The worshippers stared, waiting awkwardly, out of sorts, as he stood there. It took a long time before he finally gave up, turned away, and took a seat in the front row, next to his youngest cousin.

The flustered flock applauded meekly in confusion, a few shkoyachs of encouragement were mumbled, and Rabbi Mario said, "You've brought up a question, and next week we might even hear an answer." A few people laughed uneasily, or maybe Be'eri only imagined they did, and then somebody began to murmur the "Bameh Madlikin" chapter and the others joined in.

The next day the Shabbat left, and so did Be'eri, wandering from his uncle's home, farther into the city, through streets as long and meandering as his thoughts. In his reply, Atad had emailed that he would have to return soon—he was such a gifted researcher that he had managed to quarrel even with the documents in the library. Only now, while lamenting his father's imminent return, did Be'eri realize that he must have grown accustomed to the weekly sermons and the bedroom in Katamon. It was rather spacious, but not large enough for all the thoughts that erupted from it and at it. Trying to figure out what would change, and what he wouldn't miss, and whether this had been his final Torah portion, Be'eri walked through the cityscape full of security cameras installed by the police after the most recent Ramadan protests, and attempted to reflect back on his own life.

Wandering still, he ran into Araunah again. Her faded

tank top had been replaced with a striped dress, and the cigarette with a bottle of Belgian ale. As if she was unsurprised to see him, she said, "Day after day, huh? Well, now you've got no choice. We're going to the bar."

Indeed, he knew full well that he'd gone walking by himself with the hopes of running into someone and alleviating his sorrow. He also knew how pathetic his so-called sermon had been, and when he saw her, her rudeness of walking out in the middle seemed so justified that he allowed himself to wallow in it. Rather than think about his dad, he'd lose himself over this braless girl. Anything that distant can't really hurt.

Be'eri had turned eighteen over a year ago; despite this, he rarely went out at night, and subsisted on grape juice rather than wine during Passover. They went to the Mukataa Bar and sat inside. Araunah already seemed moderately tipsy. The servers all smiled at her, perhaps because she was pretty, or perhaps because she was a regular. She ordered a negroni, and when he asked to see a menu she ordered him a kosher cognac, and laughed when he asked the server if she could dilute it with orange juice. He downed the drink in a single gulp, like an experienced drinker or like a complete novice, and hot liquid ran out of his nose, as if he were a fire-breathing dragon. But rather than run away, she stayed. And rather than tease him until he cried, Araunah giggled along with him, ordering him a second round—a beer this time.

The beer gave him no trouble whatsoever, but her green eyes certainly did. While they talked, she presented all sorts of odd theories—that the greatest fear of desire is fulfillment, and the greatest fulfillment of desire is fear; that the two-state solution is what gets Israelis stuck, and that all they need are more nations, because then—just like Switzerland or Kenya—they'd all have to compromise. It all made a lot of sense to him, and he suggested imitating the Old City and giving a quarter of the country to the Armenians. He couldn't understand why she was enjoying his nonsense so much, and he couldn't stop picturing the braces that must have once covered her teeth—otherwise, how could they be so perfect?

Out of nowhere, she said, "You know, boys usually make the first move." He yellowed and she noticed, and rolled her eyes, and said, "What?"

He asked her why she took off in the middle of his sermon.

Seemingly embarrassed, she said she hadn't even realized he'd been speaking. Had she realized, she would have stayed. She'd left during the blessings, and had only come inside in the first place because she wanted to see the synagogue. She asked him what kind of Jews they were exactly. If they weren't reform, how come the cantor was a woman? As she saw him relaxing and letting his guard down, she ordered both of them gin chasers.

His heart was reassured. She hadn't deserted him. Or perhaps that was just the effect of the liquor. Be'eri explained that he'd been sermonizing for months, and suspected she herself might be reform. She rolled a cigarette and asked where he was headed in life, and he told her he'd always dreamed of becoming a veterinarian. She called him a kitty-cat and sided with the runaway peccary, so he decided she must be vegan too. She asked if he wanted to take a walk, and in response he asked if she was reform. She told him she wasn't Jewish, and at that moment she became even more beautiful to him— then his heart sank in shame as he began calculating his way out of their evening together.

When they started walking toward Katamon, through Independence Park, he told her how he used to love going down the slide into his mother's arms as a child. Araunah laughed, recalling how she'd feared slides as a little girl, and as if by accident, she touched the back of his arm, a few inches above his right elbow. He ignored this and asked what she was doing in the city. She pretended she hadn't touched him and told him she was working on some urban project she couldn't really discuss, something confidential, so what a shame they hadn't had a couple more drinks, she would have forgotten all about her nondisclosure agreement and would've told him everything. Her eyes suggested that they might head to another bar.

Be'eri ignored that too and, to her chagrin, asked if she was a city employee. And she wondered to herself why such a pretty guy would ask her those taxman questions, and what he was so afraid of. Well, after all, it was he who had accepted her invitation, flirted with her over a wineglass, given her the eye while she talked about the peoples of Kenya. She tried to touch him again, taking hold of his fingertips, but he saw the attached paving stones again and the scent of the wet whitewash that connected them rose up into his nostrils. This surprised him. She fidgeted impatiently as he drew away from her and searched for the perfect angle to photograph the stones.

When he returned, she told him she thought it was crazy that nothing in New York was older than three hundred, four hundred years, while here songs were chanted for every rock three thousand years ago. She looked into his eyes and ran her finger over her lips, but when Be'eri held up his screen to check out the photo, she giggled no more, feeling the wick of longing burning and burning, transforming from bated anticipation to sadness and disappointment.

She gave it another shot. She told him about a sad book

that reminded her of him, but he just kept walking among the paving stones, making sure not to step on the lines, counting his steps by threes, in his familiar sequence. Maybe something was wrong with him? Maybe he was serious when he said he didn't usually drink, and now that he'd had a bit he was already hammered? No, there was no chance he was drunk right now, he clearly moved down the sidewalk in a straight line, steadying his feet along the cracks. Rather than touch her, he continued to discover more and more attached stones, confused about the state of the streets. When he asked if the alcohol changed the sidewalks, she paused, looked at him, and said, "Oh, you."

She appeared to him full of desire, forbidden but appealing to the point of pain. She appeared to herself naked and humiliated. Typically, when people weren't interested they simply said so, and when they were, they did something about it. But what was the deal with this guy? And why was she still trying? She couldn't answer either question. She stopped him from taking any more photos, asking him to hold her bag of filter tips as she rolled herself another skinny cigarette. She'd just switched to light tobacco, so she allowed herself to smoke more in order to maintain the same blood-nicotine level. She asked if he had any brothers or sisters, but now he was so sweaty he didn't even bother answering.

He wouldn't forgive himself if he kissed her, but he couldn't just leave, either. When he fell silent, a dumb smile on his face, she smiled back at him and moved her right arm away from her body. The arm rose and her hand reached for his cheek, but he fled from her, returning to the sidewalk, moving quickly, lowering his eyes. When he finally turned back, she wasn't there.

Good. It wasn't so bad that she'd missed his sermon. Now

she was truly gone, and that, thank God, was entirely his fault. Yesterday, the day before yesterday, three nights ago, he couldn't fall asleep. He lay awake for an hour just because, then spent another hour and a half trying to figure out why he wasn't falling asleep, and another two hours being mad at himself for trying to figure out why he wasn't sleeping instead of trying to sleep. But tonight he knew exactly what was on his mind: someone had finally come along and he had scared her away. Or, rather, he had flirted with a pure gentile. In either case, his guilt was so palpable that he was convinced he'd sleep like a baby.

Drunk for the first time in his life, he spent a full hour wandering the streets. First because he was trying to gain some distance from her, then because he was trying to find his way home. He skipped over the stones, three at a time, flustered by the lines that danced along with the rest of the blurry world, ruminating on how to navigate the crosswalk he was now seeing double. Just before he got into bed, he could have sworn he'd heard a beastly wheeze, even though no one had seen roosters in Katamon in years.

The next morning, he learned that the hangover was the best part of drinking. When he was facing temptation, he suffered. But now, being punished with a headache and diarrhea in his uncle's bathroom, he finally felt worthy of his fate. Thank goodness he didn't have a shift the following day, and that he still had a few months to go before his military enlistment, and that it was so easy to claim he'd come down with a stomach bug. If he was destined to hurt himself, he'd best learn his lesson now, before he was charged with any responsibility he could sabotage.

Dr. Atad Nahumi was ready to leave thirty minutes ahead of

schedule, wrapped in the heavy rain jacket he'd bought in New Jersey, as heavy as that hot summer evening in Nayot. He'd subletted an apartment in that neighborhood while their home was still being rented out. Be'eri, however, was covered in a blanket, wearing nothing but underwear, watching for the twentieth time the clip that every news website had already shown repeatedly, the one showing the old man falling to his death from the top of a streetlight, having attempted to remove a security camera. The grandfather from Beit Safafa, whose name had remained unknown, became the Palestinian symbol of resistance to the cameras installed by the police, especially in East Jerusalem, after Jewish demonstrators at the most recent Flags March had turned violent. Over and over again, Be'eri watched the crashing camera, the old man's head hitting the pavement, the gathering crowd, the veiled women wailing.

His father grimaced at him. "People used to read the newspapers in the morning and in the evening. Now they read the news on their phones, while driving, on cranes, and they get into accidents. Is it any wonder all the news is bad?"

Dr. Atad Nahumi had returned several days earlier with two suitcases. The rest of his things were expected to arrive in a few weeks. One suitcase was dedicated to his personal effects; the other to research books and scripture. But he'd forgotten what he'd put where, and rummaged through his underwear for a while before checking the other suitcase and pulling out an interpreted Chumash from among the tomes, blowing away an imaginary film of dust. He coughed and called his son over.

"What do you want from me?" Be'eri countered. "Shabbat doesn't even start for another thirty minutes."

"I want us to prepare the sermon together, so this time

you will not shame yourself in front of those proselyte bumpkins."

"But why do I have to keep doing it? You're back now!"

"Why?" Atad thundered. "Because Professor Pitussi, that damn ravisher schmuck, is telling everyone at the Mandel Institute about the hogwash you said about the Jebusites at that Mormon synagogue of yours! You may not care about your honor, but I do."

Atad's cries made no impression on Be'eri, who continued to watch the old man falling and knew that as soon as his father walked out of the room, he'd look again at the image of the cobblestones he'd taken on that drunken night a week ago, with sorrow and a sense of missed opportunity. But Atad snatched his phone away, and opened the Chumash on Be'eri's lap to the passage that forbids marriage to the peoples of Canaan. Be'eri rolled his eyes.

"I made a mistake," he said. "It wasn't the right topic for Mario's synagogue. It was obviously not going to work. How can I explain these racist laws—"

"Racist? Oh, certainly!" Atad shook his fist. "I see that you are following in your neo-Foucauldian uncle's footsteps and insisting on applying postcolonial concepts to the days of Ezra. But before you go pick up your National Humanities Medal, let's try looking at this passage without judgment: *Their daughters shalt not take unto thy sons, for they will turn away thy sons from following me, that they may serve other gods.* Get it? No racism. They simply want to save you from idolatry!"

"But there is no desire for adultery today anyway, so what good is it?" Be'eri protested, accidentally switching *idolatry* with *adultery*. He quickly explained: "What I mean is, let's say the Torah doesn't forbid it. What's so bad about a Jew loving a Hittite if he continues to be Jewish?"

Atad looked as if he was considering slapping the Chumash over Be'eri's head. "There are more errors than words in your question, but luckily for you, Rabbi Isaac Abarbanel already asked the same thing." He passionately read the commentator's interpretation. "*And all the more, the love and bond with them shall bear no fruit. For after the Israelites took their land from their hands, those gentiles would unequivocally seek malice for Israel forevermore. Are you following this? Since you, Israel, have usurped the land from its occupants, and they are enslaved and divested of it, how could they conceivably hold you in bonds of love?* You've banished a nation under a divine decree, and now you expect to be loved?"

Be'eri stared at the video, hating his father. "Is that why you came back?" he spat. "To lecture me about assimilation? I'm not giving a sermon today."

"No problem," said Atad. "Let me know once your mind is changed. Until then, I'm keeping your cell phone."

In spite of his anger, Be'eri didn't want to just disappear from the synagogue and hurt Mario's feelings. Fifty minutes later, he walked out of the apartment with his father, no sermon in his pocket, and headed over to his uncle's synagogue and the subsequent invitation for Shabbat dinner.

And now the two of them climbed together, silent and hostile, up the stairs to Katamon, which he hadn't visited since his father's return. Be'eri asked himself where they'd be praying next Saturday. That same striped dress Araunah had worn that evening passed them by on the street and Be'eri's heart jumped, then crashed when he saw the face of another woman. He recalled their first encounter, when suddenly a prophetic intuition told him she'd be there again today, after he'd spent the entire week uneasily praying with each step to run into her, but knowing he wouldn't. All week long he'd tried and failed to track down her phone number, coming up empty with social media and search engines. He sank into obsessive thoughts: Why had she chosen him, of all people? Why did she pester him to go to a bar? She knew nothing about him, only that he was neither handsome nor ugly, so what was her deal? Maybe it had something to do with her urban project. Maybe she was just looking for a pet religious boy. But if she was a gentile, what difference did it make to her if he was observant? Why would she think of him when they couldn't have any future? He was revolted to find himself thinking along the lines of Abarbanel and took a step away from his father.

Sunset was nearing. Oddly, a boy walked past them wearing that same striped dress, and asked for directions to the grocery store in a peculiar accent.

Atad made a show of adjusting his yarmulke and growled, "I don't know the way to the grocery store, but I do know the way to hell."

Behind them, the voice of a man with a strange accent scolded Atad for his crassness. Atad was about to yell at the man, but when he turned he found his rival to be tall and solid, his muscles throbbing behind a striped dress hanging down to his thighs.

Instead of shouting, Atad only mumbled, "You won't tell me how to behave in my own neighborhood."

The man came closer and said, "No sir, *you* won't tell *us* how to behave in our own city."

Atad flinched and clung to Be'eri, who led them to a side alley that connected to Elazar HaModa'i Street. In the alley, they saw clotheslines stretched across balconies, and from all of them dangled the same striped dresses, and striped women's underwear. Men and women were chatting from balcony to balcony in a foreign language, and Atad held onto Be'eri, not because of his growing fear, but because he assumed they wouldn't bother him if he attached himself to a young man.

They walked past the basketball court by the synagogue, and did not hear the thumping of the ball, and did not see the neighborhood children. Instead they saw the foreigners' children bouncing pink tennis balls on their knees. All they had in common with the neighborhood children was the same invasive gaze they fixed on Atad and Be'eri as they passed by. And Atad kept mumbling to himself, marveling at who these people might be and what might have happened here while he'd been gone. He rushed Be'eri into the synagogue, then paused, appalled.

The entire eastern wall was covered with a stunning mosaic depicting David and Bathsheba. The redheaded king was leaning against the palace balcony, and the breasts and genitals of the bathing woman were artfully concealed by the colorful walls of Jerusalem. From the gates in the walls, the begging masses emerged in tatters, crying and howling, alongside bulls and pigs. Above, the mosaic portrayed a beautiful starless night in blues and purples and grays. And in the synagogue, alongside the regular worshippers, were whole families of the striped dress–clad foreigners. Some of the men had pointy Egyptian beards, and they conversed in their bizarre language. Even Aunt Gisella was wearing a striped dress, while Mario wore his usual shabby suit. As the rabbi walked over to hug Be'eri, his little girl showed off her new sandals. Atad was so dismayed at the mosaic that he couldn't utter a word.

"Well isn't that nice?" Mario boasted. "The conquering of Jerusalem. A new member of our community made it!

Now, take a look at the bull—an exact copy of the bull in the mosaic at the ancient synagogue in Tzippori!"

And that moment, someone summoned the rabbi from the other side of the synagogue, and that someone was Araunah; Be'eri's stomach turned. She saw him noticing her and quickly slipped out the back exit. Be'eri wanted to follow her out and demand an explanation, but that old nudnik Professor Pitussi grabbed his shoulder and started talking his ear off.

Meanwhile, Mario hushed the worshippers and announced that many community members were uncomfortable with the current wording of the prayers, and a vote on the synagogue's WhatsApp group had decided to remove the Cursing on the Heretics from the public prayer. Those who felt it important to stick to the letter of the law could recite it during whispered prayer. And Be'eri glanced at his father, who was ready to shatter into pieces of rage and dread. Professor Pitussi finally loosened his grip, and Be'eri slipped out of the synagogue and saw Araunah walking away up the street.

He followed her for a long time in quick, measured steps, trying to catch up without knowing what he'd say. The sun was setting and the streetlights turned on before his eyes. Now he was close enough to see every turn she made and he felt certain she wouldn't disappear on him. Even so, she seemed determined not to look back and rescue him from his tormenting hesitation. When he was nearly upon her, his eye caught a corner in which to hide against some stairs leading to the Moon Grove, between a building and a tree. He told himself it was a mistake to even talk to her, that she would evade him, that she would give him no answers. But it all made no difference now—whether he returned to the synagogue or continued the tracking, his father would be equally mad. And with this thought, he jumped back onto the dimly illuminated street.

While he wondered if she'd forgive him, taking three steps within the paving stones and three more on the lines, tapping his thumb to the same beat that had been soothing him since the days of kindergarten, he recalled what Araunah had told him about desire, fulfillment, and fear. He saw her dress, her sandals. She wouldn't answer if he asked her about her people. He'd have to open her mouth with subtlety. Nervous, he quickened his steps, thinking so hard he didn't notice that she'd stopped under cover of another staircase, filter tip between her lips, to pull out her tobacco pouch and roll herself a cigarette. He kept on walking until his nose bumped right into her back.

"I'm sorry, I'm sorry, I didn't see you there." He turned bright red.

Rather than getting angry, she started giggling. "What are you doing here?"

"Following you. I wanted to apologize for the other night. I had a great time, but I'm just a little confused—"

"That's a nice synagogue you've got there. I was hoping to see you."

"What are you even doing here? And how do you know Mar—"

"Hang on a sec. Hold my tobacco."

She removed the filter from her mouth and tried to roll it into the cigarette, and he recalled a book he'd read in an after-school biology class during sixth grade, which he'd hidden inside the animal encyclopedia he was always looking at. It was a guide for adolescent boys he'd found on the street and read fervently, finding in it explanations for the hair that had started sprouting from his private parts. There—in the book he'd read repeatedly until he'd finally been caught by the teacher, who told his father, who banned him from attending biology class for the rest of his life—he read in the chapter "Between Him and Her" that everything had to be consensual, but that you didn't always have to ask outright, you could just read the clues. Above an illustration of a man and a woman holding hands were examples of some such clues. Now he tried to remember what they were and if Araunah had already presented them, and what he would do if she did, and whether he was just imagining things. But even though he'd memorized the whole book, now he could only conjure a single line: *If she looks at you, smiles, and touches her lips, she must want a kiss.* He flipped through the book's pages in his mind, searching for more content, but came up empty.

Yet she liked his silence. She smiled, holding her rolled cigarette with one hand and running a finger over her lips with the other, right before her hand reached for the lighter in the tobacco pouch. He recoiled at the flame, which would desecrate everything between them, but without knowing how, his recoil transformed into closeness. Without even touching her first, his tongue was pressing against hers. They kissed and kissed and kissed. His hand in her hair, her hand running down the back of his neck.

She felt his cheek burning against hers. Judging by the crooked triangle they'd created with their stance, their shoulders touching but their feet far apart, she imagined he must be embarrassed by his erection. She clung to him anyway, making it a real embrace. He kissed her mouth, her nose. She'd dropped the cigarette long ago.

From television, Be'eri knew that the first kiss was always bad, and would make him feel as if he was being swallowed, and that breath usually smelled awful. Now he was floating, refusing to believe he'd earned the perfect first kiss. Their bodies synchronized, their breath burned, youth was hovering in midair. The only hindrance was the odd wheezing sound coming from the bushes nearby, like a tiny tractor or an intense snore. But really, apart from the strange soundtrack, he was having so much fun that he even liked this aspect, reminding him that this was really happening, right here in Jerusalem on the eve of the holy Sabbath, that he'd truly been able to attract a gorgeous girl, that he hadn't lost himself fully within delusion.

When they stopped kissing and he took her hand, his body was swept with unbearable guilt. Just like after his first time masturbating, he saw himself as the filthiest of all people. Through moist eyes, he noticed security cameras hanging all over streetlights and trees, all pointed at them, and he shuddered at the thought of the gathered evidence, yearning to smash all the cameras and all the trees and bushes that had borne witness to his deeds. When he shared this plan with her, she said, "You're funny, but I'm not that brave either. Now it's my turn to run."

And before he could fathom what she was saying, she wriggled out of his grip and skipped away. Rubbing one hand over the other that had held hers, completely unable to chase her or even move at all, he fell to the ground and sobbed.

Be'eri sat at the desk, his eyes bouncing between the dozens of books he'd spilled from his father's suitcase onto the work surface, *Mishnah* and *Gmarah*, commentaries and concordances. He noshed on some ancient matzoh that had come with the sublet, covering the desk with crumbs. Without explaining or asking for his father's help, he was absorbing every interpretation ever written about Deuteronomy 7.

Dr. Atad Nahumi, who was prepared to scream at his son for skipping prayer and dinner and making him fret, stopped short when he saw the boy, for the first time in his life, studying the Torah of his own free will. He sat down in an armchair, unsure of what to do next. The previous night, when he had wanted to protest the desecration at the synagogue, he was saddened by the thought of disrupting prayer. Later, when he wanted to go off in search of his son and never see Mario again, he was too depressed by the thought of skipping Kiddush. And now, even though he was aching to slap the child, he couldn't bear the thought of disrupting a Torah study. And so Dr. Atad Nahumi sat in the chair, noticing there was merely an hour and a half left before Shabbat ended. After a while, he gave up on his efforts to nap and decided to make himself a cup of tea. In his trembling hands, the water spilled from the samovar to the second and then the third dish and then to the floor. He couldn't stop thinking. He couldn't quell his anxiety about the people in stripes.

Every once in a while, when Atad noticed the boy pausing in his study, he would open his mouth to scold him, but just then the boy would just start flipping through the pages again. Gradually, Atad sank into the chair. The wait alleviated his fury, and he finally stopped thinking about the striped people. The smell of old paper and the sound of perusal lulled him to sleep.

When he awoke, his son was no longer home, and all that was left on the desk was a copy of Talmud Bavli open to page 54 of Masechet Yoma. Atad read:

Whensoever the Bible inscribes "to this day," the meaning is forevermore. *But is it not written in the scripture:* The Jebusites dwell with the Benjamites in Jerusalem unto this day. *The meaning here is the same: the Jebusites never vacated Jerusalem.*

Dr. Atad Nahumi did not go to synagogue, but said a quick evening prayer in the light of two stars, then rushed to check the hiding place he'd identified the day before— Be'eri's phone was gone. He called twice, yet Be'eri did not pick up. Now he walked out of the house and immediately called Mario, without saying the Havdalah prayer.

Be'eri was already on his way back to the crime scene, carrying the phone he'd removed from his father's bedside table while the man slept. He checked Facebook, Instagram, Twitter, trying different spellings, *Aravana, Arwana, Arevana, Erwana,* but nothing came up. He limped circles around the Moon Grove, where his lips had tasted hers. She wasn't there. And why would she be, if the unfounded thought that had occurred to him, and was now the only real possibility, was true?

The girl's name, same as the name of the last Jebusite king; the bully in the dress shouting at his father that the city belonged to his people; the mosaic at the synagogue depicting the refugees of Jerusalem fleeing King David . . . But even if the impossible was happening, and the Jebusites that remained in Jerusalem all along were reconquering Jerusalem now, how could a girl have kissed him so sweetly just last night, as if there were no other men in the world? In spite of his terrible guilt, and beyond the words of reproach and contempt he'd hurled at himself all night long, he knew it was too late—he was in love. It would be ridiculous to deny Abarbanel's words now—his warning that a bond of love would never rise from banishment . . . So what did she want from him?

Wandering the streets, he heard the wheezing again, growing louder, huffing and puffing. When he approached the source of the sound, he saw it: small, black, piglike.

Shmulik broke into a run, and without thinking about it, Be'eri followed. He ran and ducked among trees, panting, as if some secret sense had told him that the only witness to his love would lead him back to Araunah. Shmulik kept going, scampering and jumping and striding up the grove, flying over the wild grass of Bell Park as Be'eri hurried after him down the curving, paved path. His chest hurt and he had to pause to catch his breath. The peccary paused too, looking calm, teasing him. When Be'eri lunged at him, Shmulik flew onward, and Be'eri had a series of mild heart attacks when the peccary burst onto King David Road and almost got hit by a truck. Children screamed and cars honked, but the peccary carried on, skipping between sidewalk cracks, between boulders and monuments, Be'eri right behind him. The sweat and the stress simply revved his legs.

As he ran, Be'eri felt a vibration against his butt. He ignored it, dashing down the steps descending from the flour mill to the Sultan's Pool after the peccary, ignoring the incessant vibration—perhaps a phone call, perhaps a pulled muscle—then turning left into a narrow alley, until he bumped into somebody. Then he saw a group of young Chabadniks scattering in a panic as the peccary ran straight at them. Somebody cried, "It's a pig! It's a pig!" and somebody else cried, "It's not a pig, it's a Jebusite!" A third voice asked, "*Ober vus is Jevus?*"

The entire area was in a tizzy. In vain, the loudspeakers attempted to regroup the convention that had scattered like ripples around a stone.

And the peccary dove into Gehenna at a dizzying speed.

As Be'eri kept chase, he pulled out his phone, intending to call the police. On his locked screen, he saw six missed calls and one WhatsApp message from an unfamiliar number. *Hey, it's me, Araunah. Wanna meet RN at Moon Grove? I've got something to tell you.* This was followed by another message: *I'll be here till 10:30 p.m. I'm not sure when I'll be able to meet again.*

Heart pounding, Be'eri stopped short. His legs were frozen, unsure whether to go back in the direction he'd come from. It was ten o'clock. He knew he'd make it in time if he headed back now. He also knew that the peccary was gaining a lot of distance, approaching the Old City walls and threatening to invade the very holiest and beyond. Perhaps it was best if he didn't catch it, and just let it find its way to freedom. But Be'eri felt his legs moving at an intensifying speed, not back to where he'd come from, but forging ahead, propelled by a decisive, hopeless despair, toward the peccary. His heart collapsed in his chest, because he knew he was too weak to go meet the girl, and that she wouldn't be able to love him anyway. What did she want? Certainly not love. She must have realized he was getting closer to solving the mystery and therefore she was trying to distract him again, to use him. She knew he had found the pig and wanted to hand him over to the Jebusites. She was a Jebusite herself. Give up now and hurry to her? Huh! He'd never give her the satisfaction. Running and running down the path alongside the high walls, dropping the phone, wishing to prove to himself that he could cleanse his sins if only he took pity on the impure beast. How had he fallen prey to temptation? How could he have believed somebody wanted him? He had no choice now. He had to save Shmulik.

And as he rushed down the meandering descent into the

City of David, he glanced right, toward a grandiose illustration of Warren's Shaft on a sign outside of the site. When he looked ahead again he was startled to find Shmulik gone. How could that be? The peccary had been just a few feet ahead of him a moment ago. But Be'eri's legs were already flying down the slope and he had no reign over them. And suddenly he slipped and couldn't stop his fall into a wide crack in the sidewalk, between the stone lines. How had he not seen it? He reached out to grab the curb, but his body was already falling down into the hole. The opening was shrinking, until it disappeared from view. He realized he was dropping through complete darkness, farther and farther into a place he did not know, toward a bottom that he would hit at some point, ending his life most certainly, at age nineteen, before he could serve in the military, go to college, be an adult, before he could say goodbye to his mother and his friends.

The air grew mildewy until a glint of light flashed against the sides of the hole, and Be'eri could once again see his hands, unsuccessfully trying to grab onto something. The light was coming from beneath him now, and Be'eri peered down, and the hole had an expansive bottom, flanked by two enormous marble altars. On one of them, the wounded peccary was already bound, wheezing and squealing with terror, begging for its life, but the Jebusites ignored its pleas, blood staining their striped dresses. And the other altar was empty, and Be'eri knew he only had seconds before he would lose his life on it. The smell of blood and fire and mildew filled his nostrils; he coughed and lifted his head up.

The fall was so long he could barely breathe anymore. And he saw the hole widening, its walls embedded with television screens now, countless screens broadcasting live streams from all over the city, filmed from the security cameras installed everywhere. Be'eri saw his old home in Beit HaKerem and the Chabadniks at the Sultan's Pool and the Arabs in Shu'afat, and saw shattered glass on the sidewalk where that rioter had broken the camera, and saw Uncle Mario and his father, whom he'd never seen crying before, moving from one camera to the next, searching for him, and saw them yelling but could not hear their voices. He yelled back to his father, though Be'eri knew the man couldn't hear him, and now he saw the ground a few feet below him, and just before he lost consciousness, he saw Araunah in shorts and a tank top on one of the screens, sitting on a bench in the Moon Grove, where the cameras had punctured their kiss, hugging her knees to her chest, staring straight at the camera, waiting for him, crying.

MURDER AT SAM SPIEGEL

BY LIAT ELKAYAM

Sam Spiegel Film and Television School

L ife that summer was exceedingly simple. I didn't work out. I didn't own a television. I didn't do anything interesting and had no energy. All I had was a drug dealer named Nisso, who went to my neighbor for therapy and left some shit for me after his sessions.

It's not like Nisso ever got a shekel out of me. Back then, I had no money to spend on fun and games. Nor did I pay him with any other currency a drug dealer might find valuable, like job opportunities, blow jobs, or bullshitting. The transaction was rather simple: Nisso felt an intense urge to smoke a joint immediately après therapy, and after the grouchy neighbor from the third floor caught him bawling in the stairwell and filling the holy Talbiya air with the unmistakable sweet scent of prime White Wood ganja, Nisso had no other recourse but to be so bold as to invade the building's backyard, unaware that it belonged to the apartment owned by my grandfather, may he rest in peace.

This invasion had two outcomes. First, Nisso had to add cynophobia, fear of dogs, to his never-ending list of anxieties, although—as Dr. Porat, the psychologist from the second floor, explained to him—anxiety, by definition, means you are dealing with the unknown. If it was realistic and actually happening, it wasn't anxiety at all, but fear. In Nisso's case, it certainly wasn't the unknown that had jumped up on his chest, but a very tangible, hairy, 137-pound creature—my dog, Ash. Ash meant no harm. He only wanted to play, and interpeted Nisso's screaming as squeals of joy. By the time I emerged in the yard, wrapped in my fuzzy pink bathrobe with the bunny print, Nisso was in a posttraumatic state. I made him some herbal tea and sat him down on a tattered beanbag. After he sipped the tea and got infused with mint, and inquired as to who the yard belonged to (at his core, Nisso was a law-abiding citizen), we spent two minutes in shared silence. Then he mumbled something about his younger sister who had died, and about Dr. Porat's kinky vinyl platform shoes. Then he pulled a flawlessly rolled joint from his pocket—it looked very aerodynamic, like a rocket with wings (what the neighborhood potheads refer to as Till Eulenspiegel)—and offered me a hit. From the second puff, it was clear to me I'd arrived exactly where I wanted to be: the lost paradise of medicinal ganja.

Since then, every Monday and Thursday, Nisso would step out of his session with Dr. Porat and trudge along to his session with me, which included tea, a doobie, and some banter. The session always ended with a gesture of gratitude, embodied in a dried bouquet of three grass flowers, which Nisso tied together nicely with a red ribbon and left on my coffee table. I don't remember much of what Nisso told me over clouds of smoke. It had something to do with his deep moral dilemma about drug dealing, his intense urge to drive again (his anxiety about cars, Vespas, and other moving objects—the reason he'd originally started going to therapy— had kind of ruined his business), as well as his distinct sense that Dr. Porat was making bank from their sessions (and indeed, a year later she enclosed a balcony and treated herself to upscale Belgian profile windows).

One scorching afternoon, while Nisso exhausted me with his regular "My karma sucks, it's got me by the balls, I've sold so many hard drugs I've turned soft" spiel, his ancient beeper went off with a message from a client asking for a white shirt, which meant coke. Nisso asked me if I'd join him on a quick delivery. I said yes. It's not like I had anything better to do than count the fleas on Ash's back. The handoff was meant to take place down the street, at a local bar called Order of Capuchin. The Order, as the regulars called it, was a dimly lit, air-conditioned lair where nobody cared if I showed up early or in slippers. Carmit, the pretty bartender, would shake her overly creative cocktails and play the best of the Jackson 5 while I sipped smoky Glenlivet with a single ice cube and stared at my twisted reflection in the glass.

When we walked into the Order, Yonatan was already there, drinking a blue Jerusalem Breeze, as handsome as a young Alain Delon in *Le Cercle Rouge*. Yonatan Talmon would stop to fuel up at the Order at least once a day, at unpredictable, irregular hours. We ran into each other at all sorts of Jerusalem left-winger hangs—at parties organized by Anne and Tzahi from PacoTech, over white bean soup at Rahmo's, during protests in Sheikh Jarrah. Five years earlier we even took an existentialism class together at the Hebrew University: Davidi, Yonatan, and me. Then Davidi died, I was hospitalized, and Yonatan got into the Sam Spiegel film school—but only after his father, the justice minister, made some calls. People liked to gossip about that sort of thing—the rotten system, elitism, nepotism, and all that jazz, but for real, Yonatan was a pretty talented boy. As a filmmaker, sure, but even more so with the ladies. He always let me read the dramatic texts chicks sent him. I would swallow them down, one by one, like greasy popcorn, getting super jealous as I read, mostly jealous of the girls. Not of Yonatan and certainly not *for* Yonatan. All these girls were crazy in love with him, with an uncompromising passion that didn't leave room or air for anything else. I couldn't figure out how it happened exactly. This whole love thing seemed inconceivable to me. Way too complicated.

But not half as complicated as what went down that night, which was all my fault.

I woke up sprawled across a sticky rubber floor. I opened my eyes, but still couldn't see a thing. It was darker than black. I lifted my head and it banged against a hard surface. Some-body squealed like a slaughtered goose. It might have been me.

A few seconds later, my pupils dilated and I could tell I was in a small, enclosed room. Rolling gently left and right in an at-tempt to map the area, I realized my vision was fucked because I was underneath a titanic desk that took up half the space. Three computer screens flickered on the desk. On one screen, green numbered time lines were scrolling across; the other was stuck on a freeze-frame of an ultra-Orthodox boy chasing a cow-shaped red balloon down the alleys of the Old City; and the third screen was blinking with a Roy Lichtenstein–esque image: a Desert Eagle pistol with a white flag coming out of its smoking barrel, the word *Kaboom!* printed in red.

But that was the least of my problems.

Right there, in the corner of the room, on a swivel chair, his head hanging backward at a completely inhuman angle, was Yonatan Talmon, handsome and pale in a tight white ribbed undershirt, a long river of blood snaking from his stomach.

That was my cue to scream.

I tried to reach a vertical position, congratulated myself

on the boldness of the attempt, then dragged myself across the floor on all fours, until I managed to reach Yonatan's left leg. It was as cold as ice.

And then it hit me. I'd forgotten what it was like, but it turns out it hadn't forgotten me: the trickling of dopamine, the rise of adrenaline, the surge, and boom! In a nanosecond, I was *kanagawa oki nami ura*—under the big wave. Only today I can see how fucked up it all was: someone had to die for me to feel alive.

After that, everything turned into a fast-motion whirl-wind, a montage of panic: door opening, blinding light, gray wall. I started walking, then running. I had no idea where I was. I opened one door and found an empty, derelict class-room. The walls were covered in movie posters. When I spotted the poster for that stoner film *Blah Blah Land* for the third time, I realized I was running in circles. I was trapped in a web of twisting, low-ceilinged hallways, walking-stum-bling-running, turning a corner, walking into *Blah Blah Land* again and again. I tried to look for a new poster. I found one: at the end of the hallway was a picture of a banged-up yellow Renault 5 with a large Jerusalem stone lounging in the back-seat. Above the car was some graffiti that read: *Who stole the Wailing Wall?*

Another step, a beat, a step. A wider hallway that led to heavy, black metal doors. I pushed hard and slipped out, hit by mountain air as clear as wine. The doors slammed behind me with a terrible racket. I emerged from the bowels of a gray office building to a top-floor balcony. The sky was dark blue, a witch's moon hanging high, the kind of moon that sheds a circle of light onto the clouds around it, like a projector.

I gazed at my hands. That's what you're supposed to do if you think you might be dreaming. You can't see your own fingers in dreams, but mine were glowing red. I looked up and finally figured out where I was. Out of the blue, a pink light went on right above my head. It was a neon sign announcing, *The Sam Spiegel Film and Television School—Jerusalem.*

A peripheral, surveying glance confirmed that I was standing on a mezzanine on the third floor of a standard multilevel concrete monster in the janky Talpiot Industrial Zone. And lo and behold the wonder—slumped over four tattered orange movie theater seats, among blooming cacti and wild ferns, was none other than Nisso Ben Naim, sawing the night air with his snores.

I fished a Nobles cigarette butt from a planter, crashed onto one of the seats, pulled out the lighter eternally rolled inside the sleeve of Nisso's shirt, and lit up. If I had legs, there was no neural proof of it.

"Nisso, get up. Talmon's dead."

"Habakkuk, you can't climb up my leg, you're a fish."

"Nisso!"

"Zip it, Kiki, I'm having an incredible dream. I'm training a parrot fish."

"Nisso! C'mon, Talmon is dead, for reals."

Nisso opened one eye, revealing a hundred red capillaries. "Whatcha talkin' 'bout, Kiki?"

"His bleeding corpse is right here."

"Where?"

"Here. Inside."

"And you're just sitting and smoking? Smoking butts? Call the cops."

"Nisso, really? That's your master plan? Isn't it against the dealer's oath?"

"Shit. And I'm the last one who fed him sugar. I'm fried. Are you sure he's absolutely dead, like *dead* dead?"

"I guess he could just be casually bleeding a shit ton from his gut. Wanna go take a look?"

"I've got hemophobia. If I see blood, I pass out. It's been that way since I got injured at the Special Forces Assessment Selection."

"Dude, you were a kitchen sergeant on the adjutancy base."

"What the fuck do you know, Kiks?"

"Nothing. Especially not what happens next."

So I stared. That was something I've always excelled at. On the wall across from me was an enormous hand-painted poster of *The African Queen*. Bogart's face had been ripped off. Only the body remained. A faceless man submerged in water, swallowed by tropical vegetation undulating in a gentle breeze.

Then the machine in my head started spinning. I was back, baby, no doubt about it. I heard my pulse, as loud as if a small demon were pounding the Beastie Boys's "Sabotage" into my temples with an eleven-pound hammer.

Damn, that Mother Nature shit works.

That whole section of twisted monotonous thoughts that had been chewing up my brain for months was totally obliterated. Human existence still had no meaning, but I did: somebody had killed Yonatan Talmon, and I had to find out who. Especially since all the facts were undisputedly leading to one main suspect, and that person was none other than Riki Azulai.

AKA: me.

When we tried to get back into the school from the balcony, we found that the door had locked behind us. I wanted to race away like Road Runner, but going against my much better judgment and the clear and present danger posed to him, Nisso insisted we call the police. Since Nisso himself didn't own a phone (his main issues: police-tracing phobia and cat memes–related anxiety) and neither did I (a matter of principle: when you have a phone people think you want to communicate with them, and when I say *people*, I mean my mother), we had to get out of there and find someplace we could make the call from.

Even though I was wearing my bunny bathrobe, I suggested we go to the dance club Haoman 17, the only place in Talpiot that was still open at that time of night. That way, we could also get rid of the shit Nisso was still carrying on him. But he refused, claiming that he wouldn't "buy anything German-made, not even washing machines, and Haoman runs a Krautrock lineup tonight." He pushed his stash deep into an old five-reel projector that stood at the front of the school, right by the dark descending stairwell, the only place we could head to.

There were lots of steps back there and not much light. All of a sudden, we saw a shadowy figure ascending from the bottom of the stairs. Nisso ducked behind a wide pole covered with posters advertising an event at the Jerusalem Cinematheque: *On the other hand, of course, cinema is also a sandwich—baguette and phallus in French film.* Then a human shadow emerged on the stairwell wall, it grew larger and larger, until finally we spotted a beanie. The man climbing toward us was wearing black, humming an Umm Kulthum tune, and carrying a bucket, a mop, and a rag. It was an Arab cleaner on his way to work. We'd been living a horror movie for no reason.

We reached the entry ramp, which was sprayed with the words: *Jerusalem—a city held together with masking tape.* Nisso paused for a moment by the window of a French patisserie laden with rainbow-colored macarons. We circled the ground floor of the building to see if any of the businesses were open. We counted three bakeries, all of them closed. The sweet smell of cookies drove us nuts. I must have been having serious munchies, because usually I'm a savory kind of person.

Only then did I think of asking him: "Say, Nisso, what went down last night?"

"Word!? You don't remember?"

"I solemnly swear I do not."

As we dragged ourselves down Sam Spiegel Alley, through the concrete no-man's-land of the Talpiot Industrial Zone (on our right, Capital Construction; on our left, Ma'ase Choshev Street; and all around us, Holy Meir's Buy & Sell secondhand car lot), Nisso laid out the events of the previous night. He said that after we got shit-faced at the Order, Talmon told us he'd gotten in trouble over his final student project, a short film. According to Nisso, the movie was about a little boy whose deputy-minister father sexually abused him, and it was based on a true story. Yonatan told us that just a few hours earlier, a school committee discussed granting his film some funding, and someone must have tattled to his father, because a black government-issue BMW had been following Talmon Jr. around ever since. Nisso said Talmon had been scared and asked us to walk him back to Sam Spiegel, where he had to finish editing a trailer for a classmate's film.

Nisso and I crossed a road through a traffic island covered by a dried bed of anemones. It was the edge of the industrial zone, and apartment housing fortifications towered above standard, human boxes. Laundry hanging from barbed wire. Exposed air-conditioning units. Squares on squares. There were two hummus places in the building to the left, both terrible.

Then I heard it. It came from the pocket of my bunny robe.

"*It's just an illusion. Ooh, ooh, ooh, ooh, ahh.*" I pulled a black vibrating iPhone from my pocket. The screen showed an incoming call from *Danny—Mortal Enemy*, with an image of four men in tuxedoes on a red carpet, their arms wrapped around each other. One of them was Yonatan Talmon, two others were the Coen Brothers, and the fourth was a young man I sort of know. He looked like a 1970s German porn star. His name was Daniel Waxman, and he was Yonatan's best friend and worst nightmare. Yonatan and Daniel were both star students in their class at Sam Spiegel, friends and foes, frenemies.

"Goddamn, it's Talmon in the picture. Whose fucking phone is this?"

"His," said Nisso. "The dearly departed and recently deceased. Remember him?"

The phone kept ringing: "*Ooh, ooh, ooh, ooh, ahh. Illusion.*"

"What the fuck. Why was this in my pocket?"

"Yo, man, look at the blond guy in the pic. That's the dude who asked me to have you bring him the shit; he called it Kiki's Delivery Service, but he never paid. Go on, answer that Ashkenazi piece of shit."

But before I had a chance to answer, someone jumped on me from behind. A shivering hunk of screams and hair. There were two blows: my head against the sidewalk, and her hip bone against my head. She wrapped her thighs around my neck.

"I saw you kissing him on your feed five hours ago, you bitch. You have no clue who you're messing with here!"

"How lovely to make your acquaintance," said Nisso, examining Shira Sovarsky's long legs as they tightened around my throat. Luckily for him, Shira didn't believe in pants.

"I'm Nissan Ben Naim. And who might you be, fair maiden?"

"The love of Yonatan Talmon's life."

"May you live long and prosper and bear blond offspring," said Nisso.

While Shira kept mangling and strangling, things started to click for me, like the sound of an eighties rotary phone. Shira Sovarsky was Yonatan Talmon's ex. Queen of desperate text messages. They'd been off-again-on-again for the past thousand years or so. When Yonatan had refused to move in with her, she rented an apartment just across the street from his, in some kind of sad Mia Farrow bit that burned her heart up. She would watch from the rear window as girls went in and out of his apartment. And since Sam Spiegel students had no life whatsoever outside of school, all of these girls were her classmates. Shira had sold her car to help Yonatan fund his first short. She was the costume designer and art director for the film and gave the director blow jobs on a regular basis because he claimed that was the only thing that helped clear out his toxins. In return, Yonatan treated her like a prop and returned her with the rest of the equipment when filming was over, trading her in for the main actress, who later joined him at the Cannes Film Festival short film premiere, hosted by the Cinéfondation.

Shira continued to curse. I channeled my energies toward turning blue.

One time, Yonatan Talmon tried to hit on me too, and I think he kind of succeeded. It was at Davidi's memorial service. I threw up as soon as we walked out of the cemetery. Yonatan followed me into the bathroom and held my hair back. Then he invited me over to his place to watch the Woody Allen movie Manhattan. It was Davidi's favorite film. All throughout high school, he'd had that black-and-white movie poster tacked on his wall with the image of the Queensboro Bridge and the two protagonists sitting on a bench, looking at the city. We sat on the floor, leaning against the bed, because the sheets looked like a Rorschach test. During the bridge scene, he told me that there wasn't really a bench there. The production team had lugged two of them over. I laughed for the first time that week, and then Yonatan Talmon kissed me and I kissed him back. In the closet behind him, the clothes were folded perfectly. No way did Yonatan fold them himself. At some advanced stage, after we'd already rid ourselves of all kinds of underwear, Yonatan's phone started dancing the conga. One text and another and another. I wriggled out of his arms and glanced at the screen. It was Shira, in a hissy fit. I asked Yonatan point-blank if he and Shira were really broken up, and he babbled on about an open relationship and tried to convince me there was no reason to use condoms, either. I didn't mind that he was a liar, but when I realized he was too lazy to go down three floors to the corner store for condoms, I told him I'd go buy some and used the opportunity to peace-out into the freezing night.

Truth be told, it was the memory of Davidi that turned me on, not Yonatan.

Besides, I'd already taken a peek: Yonatan had a small dick.

Honestly, I don't normally do this sort of thing—fuck people who are in relationships. But now that Shira's silky, muscular thigh was shoved into my mouth, reminding me that I was not at all attracted to anorexic Ashkenazi chicks from hell, I truly regretted not having returned from the corner store that evening and fucking Yonatan Talmon's brains out like I know how, including a grand finale of vaginal contractions and the kind of screams that wake up the neighbors.

"So what happened last night, you fugly slut?" Shira squealed. "Did you give him head? Did you kiss him? Spill it."

"Shira, Yonatan Talmon is dead," Nisso said slowly.

Shira covered her ears with her hands and squeezed her legs around my neck like pliers.

"I swear on my life, he's dead!"

"I don't believe you!" Shira yelled, then fainted.

The sane thing to do would have been to walk Shira back to Sam Spiegel. She was shivering and crying and insisting on seeing Yonatan with her own eyes. I wanted to stay close to her, because I thought that at some point on the way over, as soon as she stopped chewing our ears off about how she and the world had lost a genius, I'd manage to get her talking about who might have murdered Yonatan. Considering what an obsessive stalker she was, there was an excellent chance Shira would be able to figure out who had done it.

The three of us dragged ourselves up the main street, full of grief and grass. Nisso paused to adjust his fireman's carry of the gutted Shira, and I tried to get her to tell me how many times Yonatan's tongue appeared on different women's feeds last night, and exactly what she knew about his movie idea and the deal with his father. Then, behind us, beyond the enormous bulletin board (A night of Torah: the honorable Rabbi Milik Shapiro discusses the mitzvah "Thou shalt not place a stumbling block before a blind man"), right in the Righteous Steak House parking lot, we spotted a shiny black BMW idling, its headlights suddenly flashing on.

Nisso and I looked at each other, then wordlessly grabbed Shira tighter and started running toward Sam Spiegel. Fortunately, the Talpiot Industrial Zone seemed like a deranged kid's Lego creation. Tunnels rising and falling, tin roofs, drainpipes, and an enormous yellow crane ruling over all, diligently constructing Hope-Hatikva Talpiot's fourth mall. It was easy enough to lose the menacing BMW and get back to the school's ramp. By that time, Shira's tears had soaked through Nisso's shirt, as she cried, "But why, for Pasolini's sake? Why?!" and then consciousness was lost, but this time it was Nisso's. It was only when we reached the black doors on the third floor that we realized we had no way of getting back inside the school.

Shira banged her fists against the doors, then paused, pulled out her phone, pouted her lips, and took a selfie. Nisso tried to jimmy the lock with a credit card, a toothpick, and a stick of gum. All of a sudden, it was like open sesame: the doors flew apart, and there he was, Daniel Waxman, platinum-blond hair, wearing all black like the angel of death, a bullet pendant around his neck and an 8mm camera on his shoulder.

"Kiki, Shira, Nisso. How do we even survive on the margins of this vortex? Talmon is gone."

Shira started screaming again and fell into his chiseled arms. Waxman cast a sidelong glance at the reflection of his biceps in the polished black doors, and started filming.

And I got in and locked the doors from the inside.

Shira and Waxman were talking. She wanted to see Yonatan's body. He objected. She insisted. He insisted harder.

"I knew this project would be the end of him," Shira gasped.

"The movie project?" said Nisso.

"All the stress around it. And that loony psychiatrist prescribing him drugs so he could sleep, eat, work. He told Yonatan it was time to kill himself for his art."

"Say what?" I blurted. I was trying to evade Waxman's camera.

"He must have killed himself, and he isn't the first or last student to do that here," Waxman whispered to me.

That was a possibility, but a low-probability one. I was surprised to hear Shira suggest it—out of all the people in the world, she should have been the first to know that no one on this planet loved himself more than Yonatan Talmon. His love for himself was so all-encompassing, so infectious, that you were forced, if only for the time you spent in his presence, to love him too. That was the secret of his outrageous charm.

"Shira, baby girl, I think he was murdered," Waxman said softly.

"Yonatan was beautiful. Yonatan was a genius. He was the future of Israeli cinema. Who would have murdered the Israeli Aki Kaurismäki?"

"Someone who likes American commercial films that actually make sense?" Waxman offered.

"His father," Nisso suggested. "Duh."

"His father?" Waxman replied. "No way. Yonatan's father worships him. It's like an Oedipus complex, except in reverse. The father wants to marry his son."

Nisso hummed. "That certainly explains some of his drug consumption."

"Yonatan told us about the sexual abuse," I said, "and how he was going to make a movie about it."

"That?" Waxman said. "That's bullshit. An old story. Yonatan was a pathological liar. Worst-case scenario, his father refused to burn tens of thousands of dollars on Yonatan's films. But he never abused him. If anything, this was Yonatan's way of abusing his father."

"Bullshit," said Nisso.

"I shit you not," said Waxman, turning the camera over. "Damn, I think I need to change the batteries."

* * *

A few hours later, when the sun took over every good patch of blue sky, the students would smell blood and celluloid and start making their way over to Sam Spiegel. The balcony would look ready to collapse with human traffic. People would document each other talking about Yonatan and argue about which backdrop was most expressive. Facebook and Twitter would blow up with personal eulogies, and that grainy black-and-white image of Yonatan wearing a tux and holding an award at some Jewish film festival would pop up on every story on Instagram. His location-study film, the one that was accepted into Cannes, would get 164,000 views on YouTube that day.

While all that was indeed happening, the police showed up at the school. A super-hot detective named Ohayon with a mustache and kind eyes locked the four of us in a classroom, and the cops pulled us out for questioning, one at a time. Nisso was the first one to be pulled out, and when he came back he was catatonic. He didn't speak a word. Waxman went next, and while he was being questioned by the police, I questioned Shira Sovarsky. She told me that Yonatan and Danny were the only two finalists for a $50,000 graduation fellowship, a one-time grant to be used for making a final project that some philanthropist was offering the graduating class. Danny's movie was about orthodox little people. It turned out there was a community of them living in the Old City, its members married off to other Jewish little people from all over the world. They were a small, tightly knit community. Shira had no idea what Yonatan's movie was about, but she knew very well that the fellowship committee had met that day and that Yonatan's movie had been chosen for the grant.

Shira believed Daniel Waxman was the killer.

When Daniel returned to the room, flanked by the hot detective on his right and a pregnant cop on his left, Shira started to scream at him: "You did it! You coldblooded murderer!!!"

As the sexy detective dragged me away, I heard Daniel calmly respond that it wasn't him. The most disturbing part of it all was his defense: "Yonatan was the best editor in our class. I really needed him for my trailer."

Detective Ohayon fixed me with a knee-buckling stare before locking me (without him, sadly) in a small editing room with a poster for the only science-fiction film in Sam Spiegel history, *First They Took the Temple Mount*, featuring a spaceship hovering above al-Aqsa Mosque. It was time for some soul searching. All my options had been eliminated. None of them could have been the murderer. Waxman knew who I was. Shira had seen me on Instagram the previous night. I was there with Yonatan Talmon in the editing room when he died and I didn't remember a single thing. And the worst part was, I knew there was a precedent. Perhaps it was time to admit the obvious truth; the lie that had started to formulate as soon as I'd woken up. It was all very much in my wheelhouse. I should know better than anyone. I had done it, and managed to hide it even from myself.

Then the door opened and my heart shrunk as if someone had bitten into it. The hot detective was standing in the doorway, holding handcuffs in one hand and his mustache in the other. Behind him, dripping blood and smiling like the Cheshire Cat, was Yonatan Talmon.

Things People Said about Me After I Died, *up-and-coming Israeli director Yonatan Talmon's first feature film, is the refreshing surprise of the Sundance Film Festival. This thought-provoking film opens with an amusing one-shot, in which a young brunette in a bunny print bathrobe is shocked to discover the bloody corpse of the auteur himself. As the film progresses, Talmon cunningly manipulates his friends and family, creating a cinematic and real-life version of that age-old fantasy: being able to hear everything those who love and hate us say about us after we die.* Things People Said about Me After I Died *is an original blend of narrative and documentary, rising from the personal to the public sphere, serving as a sharp allegory about the human mind in a postmodern world, in the days of a third industrial revolution, in which a single Instagram story is reason enough to kill a man.*

—from *Variety*

Just like everything else, summer ended.

The only thing that really bummed me out about this debacle was that now Nisso and his drugs were gone, as if the Wailing Wall Tunnel had swallowed them whole. At the end of winter, on my way to the Machane Yehuda Market, some orthodox guy jumped off the light rail, waved his arms, and cried, "Kiki!" I didn't recognize him with those long, curly sideburns, but it was Nisso.

He told me he'd quit everything, the dealing, the therapy, became observant, and went on a Chabad mission to Dnipro, Ukraine. Now he was running a local restaurant there, hocking kosher sausage. Nisso told me he had read all about Talmon's film. He wasn't angry at him anymore. On the contrary, he said. If anything, this whole mess was what had led him to find Rabbi Nachman of Breslov. He even went to see the movie, and he liked it. I told him I'd met up with

Yonatan and he'd apologized to me, mostly for not giving me very much screen time, which I didn't ask for, anyway.

"Yeah," Nisso said, "he told me that while watching the footage, he realized that even though you're Mizrahi, you came out very cold and arrogant—no one could identify with your character."

By the way, Yonatan's father was the one who ultimately funded the film, and Daniel Waxman was the editor. Daniel also hit the jackpot. *Little Orthodox People* won some prize at the Venice Film Festival. *Haaretz* published an enormous photo of him in a tux on the red carpet. At his side, shoving her way into the frame, her expression worshipful, her hair in a very tall beehive, wearing nothing but a mustard button-down ("Not a flattering color for humans," as Nisso elegantly put it), Shira Sovarsky was unmistakable.

That summer, my mother decided to sell Grandpa's apartment. Ash and I had to evacuate the green garden in Talbiya and give up the majestic avocado tree for a tiny apartment with a yard the size of two floor tiles in the Talpiot Industrial Zone. The wall we share with a car wash trembles and rattles, and is constantly wet.

But the day I left Talbiya, I climbed up one floor, politely knocked on the door, and scheduled a regular Tuesday session from now to eternity with Dr. Porat. I've been getting better ever since. I've signed up for the Sam Spiegel entry exams, and Porat says that eventually I might even be able to talk about what had happened with Davidi. In the meantime, she's gotten herself new parquet floors. It turns out white wood is all the rage these days.

PART II

CREVICES

CHRYSANTHEMUMS

BY ASAF SCHURR

Pat Junction

Outside, the mighty stars rolled through the sky, hidden from view by the soft light of the streetlamps that lined the roads. Canned laughter rose from a window, and in the yard a cat knocked over a garbage bag, a stray tin can causing the animal to scamper away. In a schoolyard not far from there, inside a wooden jungle gym, a teenager mustered his desperate courage and slipped his hand under a girl's shirt, which she allowed. After a few moments of awkward panting, his hand rose and rested upon her breast. It was as soft as he'd imagined it would be. He gasped, thinking he would pass out from the sensation of his palm against her warm skin, and she held onto his wrist, keeping his hand in place, saying nothing, only smiling at him in the dark. On the next street over, a man screamed as if he were dying, but the next moment the scream reincarnated into a throaty, stifled laugh, another voice joining in before the two fell silent. A distant window opened and slammed in the wind, a man coughed in bed, a phone started ringing and then cut off, a moped rattled away. Inside the house, however, no part of the sky could be seen and none of these sounds could be heard. And in the dream there was no one at home but him, and he was lying in bed, just like he was in real life, but in the dream a pair of eyes watched him from the doorway, and he rubbed his face with fists as crude and pungent as hunks of cured meat. In the dream, he looked at the doorway and thought, *Two girls are at the door*. Then he thought, *One girl, followed by her shadow, her hair down*.

He awoke, startled and tense. Even a moment or two later, when he'd settled down, he remained in place, unsure what had awakened him, while the knocking at the door continued. It was only a few seconds later that he realized what he was hearing, turned on the light, tented his eyes with his hands, blinked, and rushed to the door before the neighbors woke up too.

"Who is it?" he asked.

From the other side of the door, she said, "Dad! Dad, it's me! Open up! Open the door already!"

"What's wrong? Did you forget your key?" he asked, opening the door. "I thought you were supposed to stay with Mom tonight." Then he saw her face. Even her lips were pale. He startled. "What happened?" He was scared now. And angry. "What's going on? Did someone hurt you? Who hurt, you, Michali?"

"Oh God," said Michal.

He pulled her inside and closed the apartment door behind her.

"Oh God oh God oh God oh God," she cried. "I killed him, I killed him, I think I killed him."

"Killed who?" For some reason, he pictured her smiling, blushing military officer of a boyfriend, and a secret sense of victory filled him.

"I killed him, Dad," she wept. "What am I going to do now? What am I going to do?"

"Who did you kill? You didn't kill anyone, you hear me? Enough of this nonsense. You didn't kill anyone. Now come in, come into the kitchen and sit down. I'll make you something hot to drink. Does Mom know you're here?"

Michal followed him into the kitchen, plopped down onto the green Formica chair, and trembled. Her right hand, he now noticed, was wrapped tightly around something.

"What's that, Michal? What have you got there?" He took hold of her wrist, his fingertips sketching the paths of the old scars, while his other hand battled against her clenched fist until the car keys finally fell out of it.

"I did, I killed him, Dad," she repeated. "They'll put me in prison. I killed him just like that, like it was nothing. I didn't mean it, I swear. It wasn't even my fault."

At that moment, the lights went out all over the apartment.

"Don't move," he told her. "I don't want you to bump into the kettle and burn yourself, you hear? Just stay where you are. Everything's fine, okay? We just blew a fuse. We'll buy a new kettle tomorrow and everything will be fine. All right?"

He felt his way in the dark to the front door and opened it, leaving the stairwell light off. He flipped the switch in the fuse box and returned to the illuminated kitchen. Michal was still sitting there, her head in her hands. When he sat down, she looked up at him.

"There, sweetheart," he said. "See? Everything's fine. It's just that electric kettle causing a short circuit. Now you can tell me exactly what happened." He stroked the hair off her forehead and saw the mark. "What's this?"

"It was an accident," Michal said. "I didn't even see him."

"Who?"

"He just ran into the road." She burst into tears again.

The kettle, which he hadn't switched off, started steaming again. Darkness engulfed the apartment once more, but this time they both remained seated. In the meek light of streetlamps filtering through the window, he found her hand and held it.

"Where is he, Michal? Where did this happen?"

"On Hebron Road," she said, sniffing. "By the bank intersection. I didn't even see him. He just jumped into the road. I couldn't even break in time. I just couldn't. And I wasn't even going fast, Dad. I wasn't going fast. I pulled over and got out of the car right away. I got out to help him. He propped himself against the curb and I thought he was yawning or something, but these bubbles came out of his mouth, and his whole face was bloody, and his shirt. And I was alone in the car. And there was no one there to help me."

"Did you call anyone?" he whispered. "Does anyone know?"

"I didn't call anybody. Not even an ambulance. I was so frightened. I wanted to, honestly I did, but my fingers kept trembling and the phone fell and I could barely pick it up, I was shivering so bad. I didn't mean to leave him there! I didn't mean it, Dad. And Mom's car is totaled. The fender is all banged up. What are they going to do if they catch me? I wasn't even drinking. I barely even had anything to drink. We have to go to the police. Do we have to go to the police, Daddy?"

"Now you listen to me," he said. "Listen carefully. You were alone in the car, right?"

Michal nodded.

"Did anyone see you? Could you tell if anyone saw you?"

She shook her head.

"And where's the car? Is it back there?"

"I parked it next to a demolition container," she said, her pale face suddenly turning red. "I left it right up against the container, the fender almost touching it. You can barely see it. But it's not like I was trying to hide it or anything."

"What container? On the *street*?! Where's your head? In the middle of Hebron Road, where all the police cars drive by? It'll be light out in four hours. The place must already be crawling with cops. Oh, Michali."

"Not there," she said. Even in the dark of the room, he noticed her rubbing the fingers of her right hand over and over on her palm. Then she placed her left hand on the table and stared at it. A moth slammed into the window, its shadow wings fluttering over the back of her hand. "In the lot behind Haim's barbershop."

"You drove all the way there in a banged-up car?"

"I drove as far as I dared, and then a car came up behind me and I thought, *What if the guy goes around me and looks in his rearview mirror and sees my broken headlight?* Everything was all bent. So I just turned and then I saw the container and pulled up. I didn't mean to just leave him there and not even call an ambulance. I'm not that kind of person. I just panicked, and I couldn't use my phone. Everything kept slipping. Don't hate me."

He waved her off impatiently. "Text Mom," he said. "On the phone, right now, before she wakes up and finds you gone and calls the police or something. You know what she's like. Text her that everything's fine—you forgot the keys to her place so you decided to spend the night here. I'll take care of everything else, understand?"

Michal nodded.

Now he saw that her pants were stained. She must have kneeled in the puddle of blood on the road.

"Use a pair of my pajamas," he said. "Give me your pants. I'll throw them out on my way."

He looked away as she stood up and removed her pants, but still glimpsed her underwear, printed with balloons and cartoon characters. Before he slipped the pants into a plastic bag, he turned them over and had a look. There was no blood in the back. *Maybe the upholstery on the car seat is clean*, he thought. "You didn't leave anything in your pockets?" he asked, then went ahead and checked them himself.

An ambulance wailed out on the street, the red lights flickering on the wall of the building across the road. They looked at each other.

"I'm leaving my phone here," he said, "so don't try to call me. And don't open the door. No matter who comes by, don't answer them and don't open the door. And don't call anybody. Don't touch your phone. Text Mom and then don't touch your phone again under any circumstances. Just put it on silent, okay? And don't pick up if anyone calls. Even if it's Mom. Don't tell her a thing, you hear? And don't call what's-his-face."

"Yariv."

"Yariv. And we're never going to discuss this ever again. Swear to me. After tonight, we'll never breathe a word of this. Not to Mom or your friends or what's-his-face, or your husband when you get married, or the children you'll have, God willing, or anyone else, ever. Neither of us will. Not a word to anyone, understand? Ever. Not even to me. I'll take care of everything, and starting when I get back we won't talk about this again. It never happened. None of it."

His footsteps echoed through the stairwell, though he tried to be silent. There was no one out on the street. Across the road, a lamp flickered, then went out. He walked with his head lowered. The headlights of a car appeared on a nearby street and he rushed into a building's entrance, holding his breath, until the light bathed the mailboxes outside and then disappeared. A minute or two later, a man wearing a wrinkled military uniform walked out of another building soundlessly, a large knapsack over his shoulder, and nodded at him in the camaraderie of those who are awake late at night. He smiled strenuously and nodded back. Just after they passed each other, he heard an engine sputtering, followed by the awful thunder of music emanating at full volume from a car that had just been started, then a brief burst of cursing, then silence. As the car drove past him, the driver smiled apologetically from his window.

When three giggling girls walked toward him, he quickly sat down on a stone wall and buried his face in his hands. Two of them made faces and shushed each other drunkenly, while a third, leading the way, raised a hand to silence them as she spoke into her phone. Who was she speaking to this late at night? he wondered, waiting for them to pass, hoping they wouldn't look his way. "You're a silly brat!" the girl announced as they drew closer. Through the cracks between his fingers he saw her pulling the phone away from her ear for a moment, her lips curling indulgently. "You're a silly brat and a rascal and you're uninvited tomorrow night. I'm taking back your invitation . . . No, I'm kidding, I'm just kidding, of course you're invited. I miss you, I'll see you, I love you, and tell Yogev he has to come with you or I'm never talking to him again, ever, ever, in my life . . . Okay, okay, go to sleep already, bye."

He waited for them to move away and glanced to make sure they weren't turning around to look at him. Five minutes later, he sat down again, this time on a wall across from the dirt lot. He sat there, staring at the car. No one was on the street. No one was watching him. He got up and crossed the road, prepared to flee, to play innocent, or to take full blame if police officers hiding inside of the container or in a nearby house suddenly lunged at him. But nobody did.

He walked over as if he was just a curious pedestrian. He feigned interest in the dirt, kicking a rock, as if he'd just happened on this lot by chance. He looked around like a man strolling casually to stretch his legs, and circled the car. The damage was significant, yet limited to the fender and the hood. The right headlight was broken. The windshield was intact. Even the license plate was unharmed. Inside, the contents of the glove compartment were scattered on the floor: dusty sunglasses, a pack of tissues, old cassette tapes that no one listened to or could listen to anymore. Years ago, Aviva had installed a CD player in place of the old tape deck that had come with the car when they'd bought it together.

He glanced at his watch. In three hours, the sun would be coming up.

Whenever a car passed on the road, he raised his hands to hide his face, pretending to blow on them for warmth, though the night wasn't particularly cold. He ran until he feared he would become breathless and fall down, then continued in a brisk walk, head lowered, then ran again downhill until he reached the intersection. He walked past the locked metal grate of the falafel shop and something soft smooshed under his feet—a white paper bag, streaks of tahini and chopped salad smearing on his shoe. Terrible rage suddenly filled him and he felt like punching someone. At the traffic light up ahead, two white cars sped by, flush up against each other. In the other direction, a moped stood at the red light. In the silence of the night, he heard the driver's laughter bursting, small and stifled, from within his helmet. The guy must have been talking on his phone.

He ran across the empty street. When he reached the other side, he looked back. The tracks of a single foot, sketched in tahini, faded gradually and disappeared halfway across the road. He turned onto the path and walked past an open trash can. A sudden gust of wind shifted the plastic hanging off empty cardboard soda can cases that rested on the asphalt. The smell of old pickles haunted the place like a ghost.

He felt like going up to the second floor, to their old apartment. He didn't, of course. The stairwell had been re-painted at least twice since then. Nothing remained on the walls. But when he looked up, he thought he could still spot the smoke stains on the ceiling, even after all these years. He knocked softly on the door of the first-floor apartment. Then he knocked again, harder.

"What?" a voice inside moaned. "It's two in the morning. Who died? Goddamnit."

He knocked again.

"Yossi," the voice inside whispered furiously, "if this is more of your bullshit, I swear to God I'll come out there and fuck you up. Go sleep in a trash can, you son of a bitch."

He knocked again.

The door flew open. Gabby stared at him, his hand still on the doorknob.

"I killed someone," Nahum said.

Gabby turned sideways and Nahum walked in. The place was exactly as he'd remembered it. The walls hadn't been painted. Even the plastic clock remained on its spot on the wall, with its unmoving pink hands and dirty pink frame. A ratty blanket was bunched at the edge of the couch. A few empty cups decorated the coffee table—he still remembered how his father had brought that table home one Friday afternoon, set it in front of the television, and patted it as if it were a loyal horse or dog—alongside some stacked dirty plates and an open bottle of Coke.

Gabby closed the door.

"I killed someone," Nahum said again. "I ran him over. In Aviva's car. An '87 Ford Fiesta. The fender is totaled, and the right headlight is gone."

Gabby stared at him, blinked, then ran his hand over his cheek, as if trying to assess how urgently he needed to shave.

"It's going to be daylight in two and a half hours," said Nahum. "The police will find it, easy. So I came here. It's five minutes away."

"So you thought, *Gabby's a criminal, he'll know what to do?*"

Nahum leaned against the wall. All of a sudden, he realized how tired he was. "You used to have that friend with the tow truck," he said. "That's why I thought about you."

"He left the country," Gabby said. "The IRS was on his case. Wanted half a million shekels. He sold the truck and moved to Canada." He picked up a pair of pants from the floor and pulled a cell phone from the pocket. "You're lucky I have a good head on my shoulders." He clicked the phone alive. "And that Effy's wife is in Turkey with her sister."

"Who's Effy?"

"What difference does it make?" said Gabby. "He's got a tow truck, and his wife isn't around to nag him about who's calling him at two in the morning. That's all you should care about." He raised a hand to silence Nahum, who wasn't about to say anything, anyway. "Effy, you piece of shit!" he said into the phone. "Yes, I know what time it is. You think I'd call you in the middle of the night if it wasn't important? My car's dead. Can I borrow your tow? I'll bring it back in two hours." He reached a hand over to the coffee table, picked up a cigarette, and lit it. "There you go," he said, hanging up. He sat down in an old recliner and coughed deeply. "Everything's fine."

"How is everything fine?" Nahum cried. "A man is dead, do you get it? A man is dead, and all you can say is everything's fine? Aren't you even going to ask me what happened?"

Gabby shrugged. "I haven't seen you in twelve years and all of a sudden you show up at two in the morning. What are you looking for, a heart-to-heart? You want to talk, talk. Just don't bullshit me."

"What?"

"*What?*" Gabby repeated. "Who did you run over, huh? You didn't run over anybody. You rolled out of bed barely five minutes ago, your hair all crooked. What, you think I can't tell?"

Nahum bit his lips.

"Who did it? Aviva?" Gabby got up and grabbed his keys from the table in the small kitchen.

"I wouldn't come to you for Aviva," said Nahum.

Gabby paused. "Michal, huh?" he finally said. "I never would have imagined. In my mind, she's still a little girl." A girl who, in his imagination, still wore a scrunchie in her carefully brushed hair, which would be tousled when she woke up from a bad dream in the middle of the night. He smiled and shook his head. Then his smile disappeared. They stood there, looking at each other. "Come on," he said, "let's get the tow truck."

"Aren't you going to lock up?" Nahum asked when they were out in the stairwell.

"What's there to steal?" Gabby shrugged. "So, how's Mom?"

Nahum shrugged too. "She's not fully there anymore. I try to come see her once a week, when I can make it work."

Gabby nodded.

"Last week she thought I was you," Nahum said. "I didn't correct her. It's best if she thinks we both come visit. Not that it matters. She forgets everything anyway."

They walked quickly. Gabby dropped his cigarette butt, which continued to burn on the sidewalk behind them. "You didn't have to do that," he said. "If I'm the piece of shit, let me be the piece of shit. Besides, what kind of person can't tell their children apart?"

They both fell silent for a moment.

"I didn't mean it like that," said Gabby. "I wasn't talking about you. It's not the same thing. Obviously."

To their left, at the edge of the street, they spotted the tow truck, parked partially on the sidewalk. A man was leaning against it, watching them. A bitter taste filled Nahum's throat and he walked to the side of the path to spit. Chrysanthemums struggled to break through the dirt, like fingers with more fingers sprouting out of them, all reaching out to caress something unseen.

"I guess the world couldn't get enough of your ugly face so it decided to make another one just like it, huh?" Effy said as he handed over the keys.

Gabby and Nahum glanced at each other.

"You didn't need to come downstairs," Gabby said.

"I wanted to save you the trip up," Effy replied. "You want me to come with?"

"No, it's fine. My car just died."

Effy gave him a long look. "At three o'clock in the morning," he said. "Fine, fine, I'm not asking any questions."

"Where'd you say the car was?" Gabby asked.

"Bethlehem Road," Nahum said. "Keep straight on Oranim and take a left on Judea."

"You couldn't find a spot with even more cops sniffing around? God bless you. Did you at least remove the license plate?"

Nahum said nothing.

Gabby nodded emphatically. "Fine, we'll hurry up then."

They drove silently through the empty streets. At the top of a hill, a pockmarked teenager rode toward them on his bicycle, going against traffic, and waved happily.

"Friend of yours?" asked Gabby.

"I don't know him," said Nahum.

Gabby took a long look at the Fiesta. "Hood, fender, and right headlight," he concluded. "How long do we have?"

"Two hours till daylight," said Nahum. "And Aviva needs to have the car by eight."

"That's fine." Gabby winched the car to the tow truck and they were on their way. Silence again.

"You know, I thought about growing out my beard," Gabby suddenly said. "Then I thought, no, you must have decided to do that too, so you wouldn't have to look in the mirror every morning and see my face."

They pulled up outside the barbed-wire fence, got out of the truck, and peered into the lot. Battered cars were piled up in rows across the dirt.

"There," Gabby pointed. "Same color, same everything. There's a toolbox in my backseat, go get it."

After Nahum retrieved the toolbox, Gabby grabbed onto the fence and lifted his left leg in the air. "Give me a boost. Remember how we used to do it?"

Nahum linked his fingers together and ducked down to help Gabby up. "Don't start that now," he said. Gabby was quickly on the other side of the fence, holding on with one hand and reaching the other toward Nahum, who passed him the toolbox. "I'm not here to get nostalgic," he said. "Get it, Gabby? I'm not here to get nostalgic and I'm not here to play soccer. I'm here for Michali. That's it."

Gabby said nothing. He worked quickly and silently. When he was finished, he stacked two empty plastic crates on the shaded side of the lot, climbed up, and passed the fender to Nahum. Then he dropped the headlight into Nahum's hands too. "You're the one who's got it wrong," he said, struggling to hoist the hood over the fence.

"Fuck you, Gabby."

"You're the one who's got it wrong," Gabby repeated. The crates abruptly collapsed underneath him and the hood clanged down to the ground. They both froze. A few seconds went by and no sound came. Gabby stacked the crates again.

"All you had to do was keep her outside," said Nahum. "I went in. I went right into the fire. All you had to do was make sure she didn't come in after me. That was it."

"She was right there," Gabby said, "then she was just gone. I thought she ran into the road, you see? I ran out there to make sure she didn't get hit by a car. I never imagined she went back inside."

"I could have gotten both of them out, Gabby," said Nahum. "Just stand on the sidewalk and hold her hand so she wouldn't run back inside. That's all you had to do."

Gabby said nothing. They got back in the truck.

"Instead, I see her standing there at the door in her pajamas," Nahum continued a few minutes later, when they pulled up to the old building again. "They weren't even wearing the same pajamas, you know? They weren't even wearing the same clothes. But her sleeve was already on fire, and I didn't even think about it. What kind of father can't tell his girls apart? You tell me. I rescued the same kid twice. All you had to do was keep her outside, that's all. How did you expect me to look you in the face after that?"

By the time they finished, the sky was getting brighter.

Gabby slammed the hood shut and went to screw the license plates back on. Nahum got in the car and turned the key. The engine sputtered but didn't start. He tried again.

"You're going to flood it," said Gabby. "You don't have a light touch."

Nahum got out and let Gabby into the driver's seat.

Gabby had the car started in no time. "Here we go!" he thundered like an announcer. He stepped out of the car, grabbed a hose that was rolled up in the corner of the yard, and sprayed the whole car with water. Then he sat back down in the driver's seat and turned on the headlights.

"Does the right headlight work?" he asked.

Nahum walked to the front of the car and his enormous shadow hunched against the wall of the building like a primordial giant. "It works," he said.

"Fantastic." Gabby gestured for Nahum to stand back, then took three fast spins through the dusty yard. "There," he said, stepping out and pointing at the mud covering the sides of the car with casual pride. "No one would even dream this car was fixed up last night. You can't tell the difference. You just can't tell."

Nahum slipped the car keys into Aviva's mailbox. When he got home, he'd call and tell her he'd dropped the car off for her on his way to work.

He walked out of the building and sighed. When he moved past the car, he reached out and patted its roof, as if it were a horse. A girl jogged past him, huffing, without glancing in his direction. Her ankles were thin and her calves were thick as thighs. His gaze followed her as she drew away, swinging inside of her rolls of fat like a skinny person running inside of another, larger person.

When he reached the end of the street he looked down at the valley. A pale layer of fog rested over it, as if it were a board that a tired teacher had tried to wipe clean, instead raising clouds of dust all around. The boys in the back row would cough emphatically, making a scene. The air in the classroom would already be heavy with the odor of hormonal sweat.

He walked home like a somnambulist. He didn't think about the direction, only about his feet. A boy and a girl passed him, hand in hand, wild-haired and blushing. The city was waking up slowly with the help of alarm clocks and garbage trucks. A man and a woman sat silently at a table on a balcony, sharing a cigarette. When Nahum stepped into the road without looking, an ambulance sped around the corner and honked madly, veering away at the last minute. The paramedic sitting in the passenger seat glared at him and shook his fist as they blew past. As the ambulance rode away, the red lights flashed on building walls like a flame.

Nahum looked up to the thin strip of dawn marking its

path over the neighborhood. No squad cars were waiting out-side his building. No one was lurking in the stairwell. A light went on in the second floor, his bathroom window, then im-mediately went off again. The kettle must have boiled.

TOP OF THE STAIRS

BY YARDENNE GREENSPAN

Yemin Moshe

At eight a.m. on a Tuesday in April, Abe Melkin opens his eyes and needs to write. He hasn't felt the urge in weeks, like a delicate needle scraping the universe underneath his skin. But there it is now, a choked whisper through the static filling the space between his ears—*Write.*

But first: the colossal effort of rousing his arm, of lifting it up and reaching it over to nudge Rachel awake. This is essential for getting him down the marble stairs and through the elongated dining room into his office. He needs her body, clutched against his, to carry him down. Sometimes, in the middle of the night, he startles awake and wonders where his own body has gone. Heavy and rotund, with a gut that threatens to burst his shirt buttons and a tread that used to drive students back to their seats, it no longer feels real to him. It is her body, aged yet lithe, the smooth, thinning tan skin with its dark freckles, that he believes in.

The house was just a pile of bricks when they moved to the neighborhood of Yemin Moshe in the 1970s, not the gentrifiers themselves, but those who benefitted from the outcome without having to see the trauma with their own eyes. He spent months working on the house. Well, supervising, mostly. He was already a university professor, lifetimes away from his pioneering days, before the war, when he built the road leading to a kibbutz in the Western Galilee. *But I pitched in*, a disgruntled voice fumes inside his head. *Sure*, the static in his head mocks, *you laid down one brick for a photo op.* Yes, the construction workers were patient enough to let him set down a brick or two as Rachel snapped a photo. *Never mind*, the voice insists meekly, the fury too tired. It was his. *His.*

Abe and Rachel had decided on an unusual floor plan that he admired—the bedrooms on the ground floor and the rest of the house down the stairs. The structure matched the topography of the neighborhood, built on the slope of a mountain, the streets leveled on planes. Over the years, whenever he wasn't teaching or holding office hours, Abe spent hours in his study or the living room, looking through the window toward the old city across the valley. He preferred his airy home to the stuffy office for conducting research. The landscape was no less part of his writing process than the old typewriter—later replaced with a basic word processor—or the tomes on the history of Thessaloniki or the Jews of the Middle Ages. With time, he had spread out from his study, often preferring the long, sturdy butcher-block dining room table as his workspace. The books and loose leaves of paper fanned out over the hard birch, and Rachel let him use it up. Walking down the marble stairs to what had metastasized into an unending office, every footstep spoke his pride and ownership. *His.*

But the past five years have taken something he cannot name. The blood circulating through him has neglected his legs, which grow painful and swollen by the day. Unreliable. At ninety-one years of age, he tumbles, gut first. *Weak*, the static in his head offers. No recourse but to be picked up by his wife, so much smaller than he, not much younger. He admired her all these years for her strength and athleticism, for joining him as he ventured between fellowships and teaching appointments around the world, traveling and studying in far-flung locales, slipping in and out of temporary lives, allowing him the time and room he needed to work. But watching from the ground as she pulls him up onto his feet, he thinks, *Follow me around. No, she was stealing my lead. She with her body that somehow keeps shaking off the years.* When her dark hair hides her face as she leans over him, supporting his back with one hand and pulling him by the arm with another, he can hardly even recognize her.

Now, in bed, when he finds the power to move his arm and tap her on the shoulder, she slips out and around the bed to help him up without a word, as if it was just another part of sleep.

The screen flashes an unfinished paragraph at Abe: his arrival at Venice's oldest synagogue immediately after the city's liberation at the end of World War II, as part of the Jewish Brigade of the British military. That April day must have been bright as he climbed up the crumbling stone steps with the rest of his troop—the very first Jews to set foot in the place after years of occupation—but as he closes his eyes to recall the scene, what he sees are gray clouds, weighty with doom. "Step lightly!" they kept rebuking one another. "You can break your neck on these things!" But really, they were racing up those stairs, their hearts leaping, they couldn't help themselves, to the heavy wooden doors. The city groaned with their presence, smelling of its usual standing-water dankness, exacerbated by years of stagnation under threat of bombing. They pushed the doors open and walked into the dust. The place had been pillaged and used for ammunition storage, but part of the painted windows survived, the bima was still standing. They couldn't stop touching everything, confirming it with their fingertips. They converged again in front of the Torah ark. Silently, they looked to Abe, who knew what he had to do.

Looked to you, did they? the static in his head needles.

Yes, they looked to him. He grinds his teeth. He was the only one brave enough to gently move the red curtain and peek behind. He writes that down. He does not write down: *When I touched the curtain I felt my body melting into nothing.*

"It's here," he said back then, voice breaking. He reached in and removed the Torah scrolls from the ark. Spreading them open, he turned around, facing Jerusalem.

The next day, the brigadier general went in with journalists and photographers to do the same thing in his official capacity. Smiling at the camera, he opened the door, he touched the painted windows, he brushed the curtain aside, he carried the Torah. He liberated the synagogue for the world to see. No one ever knew that Abe and his fellow troops had been there first.

Does it matter? the static wants to know.

"Yes, it fucking matters!" Abe barks under his breath, eyes widening with surprise at the sound of his own voice. He pauses. Listens. No stirring from the rest of the house. She hasn't heard.

We left the synagogue, and then what? What happened then? Abe's fingers creak slowly across the keyboard, his mind screams all his histories at him, and for the life of him he can't tell what followed. All the years of fighting, of learning and teaching, buzz in his ears. The constant reading and writing, the essays and the books, the theses, they burn in his retinas. In his heart, images mash up and twist about: Lying on the floor of the shack he rented from an elderly woman in the Galilee, burning with dysentery, all alone. His older sister, Atalja, in Paris, translucent and emaciated after years in a Siberian labor camp, gnawing on a whole sausage. He sees himself in Dir Yasin, picking up Arab bodies killed by other Israeli soldiers, and then running up to his commander, out of control, bawling the injustice at him, spitting out screams; and at the same time he sees himself sitting on his army cot in the Libyan desert with his head in his hands, having just learned that, in Europe, his parents and younger sister had been shot in the street.

He stares dumbfounded as these collages blot and stain his field of vision. He never should have gone back, he thinks. *Back where? To Europe? To writing?* He had to. His fingers piano over the keys, too gently to actually hit them. He doesn't know what came first. What led to what. His eyes stare through the bright screen and finally close with a flutter of the lids.

At some point, Abe can't tell when—*does it matter?*—there is toast, tea, and a buffet of medication: blood thinners, ACE inhibitors, thyroid balancers, whatever's on the menu for today. On the kitchen wall, a pad reminds him of how long it has been since he played any practical role in this house—an old grocery list that Rachel made him five years ago, when he thought he might still make it to the store. Milk, eggs, challah. Forever.

When breakfast is over, he must go through the indignity of their morning walk. Rachel leads Abe up the stairs from the dining room to the hallway, and sculpts his body into a leaning position: back against the banister, hand supported by the entry table, where she fiddles with the house keys. When she is ready for him, she picks up his arm and links it with hers, and they step out of the house, closing the heavy wooden door behind them but leaving the iron gate open. They always keep it open when going on short outings.

Rachel's hair covers her face again as she studies the ground like a diligent ant. The paths are paved with Jerusalem stone, full of lethally uneven dips and swells. He cannot see her face as she scours the ground for hazards, with him leaning against her arm, eyes torn at the neighborhood around him.

There are no roads in Yemin Moshe; no vehicles. Hardly any pedestrians. After the Mizrahi residents were expelled in favor of Ashkenazi intellectuals, the latter began to sell their homes to international expatriates who were charmed by the peacefulness, the Arab-style architecture, the elitism that washes over everything. These expats made the once-lively homes into their vacation houses, empty other than during summertime. Outside Yemin Moshe is a new world, bustling with the honks of cars and the beeping of cell phones. But within the confines of Abe's life there is holy silence. The pointy protrusions through the soles of his shoes; the ancient whiteness all around him: the whole neighborhood feels coated with antique, scratchy marble. Abe looks at the thick trunks of the fig trees, the black metal gratings, the vines snaking up white stone houses with red-tile roofs; at the small Armenian painted plates attached to the walls of houses, the residents' names engraved in curved, Aramaic-style Hebrew lettering. He feels the wind blowing through his bushes of white hair—*whose bushes of white hair?*—and on the other side of the small valley he sees the walls of the Old City blazing in the sun. *Blazing? Isn't it January?*

It was January when they took her, the static in his head chimes in.

Abe shudders. *January? Took her?*

"All right?" Rachel asks.

He grunts a response. She pulls on his arm gently, steering him back around. Time to take his body home.

Rachel deposits Abe in his armchair in the living room. She makes him a glass of dark black tea with lots of sugar and lemon slices and places it on the table, within arm's reach. *She doesn't even ask if you want it,* the static notes. *Just tells you that you do.*

"I'm going to the market," she says. "You'll stay right here?"

"You don't need to worry." *Go already.*

When she is out the door, he picks up the tea. His fingers refuse to cooperate and the cup dances around in his hand, the tea splashing onto the belly of his shirt. He is sure it is boiling hot, but he can barely even feel it.

Black tea, just like she used to take it.

She? But how could he possibly remember? He shakes the thought off.

"Every single day," he mutters, dabbing at his shirt with the back of his hand. He puts the cup back on the table and picks up his book. He reads for a few minutes before dozing off.

When he opens his eyes, something isn't right. The living room, covered from top to bottom with art and history, is not his. He glances down at his chest, his gut peeking out between shirt buttons, his slacks with the yellowing seam, the socks spilling down ankles, the soles of his shoes softened with weight. The clothes of an aging intellectual. Not his. He has only ever worn his play clothes, his youth movement uniform, military fatigues. Perhaps he dressed up in costume to make his baby sister laugh? *Where is she, anyway?* He was supposed to watch her. *Mother will be cross.*

But this can't be where he lives. He looks around. Oil paintings, stone sculptures, collectibles from India and Greece that he's only seen in his father's history books. *Whose home is this?* Clouds pregnant with rain hang heavy like fruit outside the window. Fists push into the seat of the chair to lift his colossal mass and his fingers skip and flutter until they finally grab at the handgrip of his cane. He smells salt and standing water. *January is when they took her. But if it's January, then where is the snow?*

He goes to the window and looks outside, at the afternoon sun shining over the wall of the Old City, over the Tower of David. *It looks like Jerusalem.* He remembers being here briefly before the war, but then that didn't really count, did it?

"Elza?" Nothing. He's already too late. They've already taken her. Or perhaps she's managed to escape. He knows he was with her earlier today, but he never saw her face. Dark hair. They went for a walk outside. *Outside! That must be where she is.*

He is not prepared for how long it takes to get to the marble steps by himself. How does he usually do it? Does his mother help him? Though this isn't his home, he somehow knows, when he reaches the bottom of the stairs, that the door is up there, and he knows where the keys lie on the entry table beside it. He knows that the small key locks the heavy wooden door and that the larger, silver one locks the iron gate. He can't quite conjure the warmth of the wood and the cool of the iron on his trembling fingers, but knows he's been led out through them.

He can't say exactly how he makes it up those stairs. Each

lift of the leg is like pushing a boulder up a mountain. The banister grows slippery under the sweat from his shaky palm. At one point, he is aware that he is crawling up, like a baby, like his baby sister. Dark hair on her face. He has to make it up there if he's going to find her. She is out on the street. *They called her out into the street.* He wasn't there anymore when it happened. He'd already gotten out.

At the top of the stairs, he leans himself against the banister, one hand propped against the entry table. Why does he do this? Who taught him? When he looks up, he sees an old man in the mirror. He gasps. *Who is that?* Is he the one who took his sister? His sister . . . why can't he picture her face? All he can see when he imagines her is a dark curtain of hair and—

No, the static says, *you've got it all wrong.*

Abe's eyes flit over the keys on the entry table, the shawl hanging on a hook, the cat's-eye sunglasses in a small tray. A dark curtain of hair. That's not his sister! That's *her!* His so-called caretaker, the woman who calls herself Rachel, calls herself his wife. The one who pushes him around from one place to the next, feeding him who knows what kinds of medications—

Which is it, then? Is the woman with the curtain of dark hair Rachel or Elza? *When faced with multiple theories that can explain a scenario, one must utilize the scientific method in order to assess*—but how does he know this? He didn't learn this at school.

He looks up at the mirror again, and he sees him. The boy he was. The boy he is. Blue eyes, blond hair, smooth, sun-kissed arms. Avram Melkinsky. He lives at 13 Żydowska Street, in the Polish town of Tarnów, not too far from the synagogue. Now he is certain: the woman who calls herself

Rachel is a menace. She has taken his sister. He will go and retrieve what is his. *His.*

He steps out of the house and locks the wooden door as well as the iron gate behind him. He will not be coming back to this house.

But outside the house nothing is clearer. The white, jagged pavement; the still, heavy houses. It is like a silent hallucination, all this brightness closing in on him. The sun scorching the back of his neck, his exposed scalp—*where'd the hair go?*—strange weather for January. *And it must be January*, he reminds himself, *because that's when they took her.*

When she took her, the static corrects.

His legs are like the ships docked on the shores of Tripoli. Lifting them takes everything he's got. Strange that a young boy's body can feel this impossible to move. But he must move, must find Elza. *They took her out into the street.*

Oh, but how can he find her when the street looks so different? No butcher shops or tanneries. No ladies in furs. No Polish military barracks. All he sees are the jagged tiles, the ornate bars on windows, the stairs, stairs everywhere. Whenever he thinks he has found his footing on the pointy tiles, they erupt to make way for a tree trunk tumoring out of the ground, and he has to grab the rough bark for balance. It does not feel like Tarnów at all. He follows the glare of the sun and sees the Tower of David in the distance, across the Valley of Hinnom—*Valley of Hell*, the static translates—twinkling him blind.

Jerusalem! But what would he be doing in Jerusalem? Yes, he went there before the war. He was the first in his family to make the promised journey to Palestine. Well, of course he did! He came to build a home for them all. But he went back when the war started. He fought in Libya first, driving through the desert in a military jeep. Then he went to Italy and taught all those small Jewish children how to read and write. But it was all for a cause. He came to save them! Surely he'd gone back to save them. He brought his older sister Atalja back, did he not? Once he was able to get her out of that Siberian camp. Surely he'd gone back for Elza as well.

Then what would he still be doing in Jerusalem? Perhaps he was only dreaming he was in Jerusalem. Holy dreams. But no, the nameplates on houses bear Hebrew lettering. He can read Hebrew, he learned it at synagogue.

The synagogue! The synagogue is just a short walk away from their home in Tarnów. That must be where Elza was taken. It was only logical—the Jews were rounded up in the synagogue.

He knows how to get there. It is up the stairs. And yes, the stairs here might look different, more like the ones that lead to the Sephardic synagogue of Yemin Moshe—he must remember this from *before*—but he knows they will lead him to the synagogue and that's what matters.

How to get up there? He tries to lift one foot after the other, but unlike back at that house, here he cannot make any headway. The stairs are too steep, the stone too slippery. He takes hold of the vines that crawl up the wall alongside the stairs and starts pulling himself up. There are thorns on the vines that pierce through his skin, allowing the vines to seed themselves into his flesh, planting him into this place, sprouting him up, one step at a time.

Twice he almost falls—one foot tripping the other. "Step lightly," he whispers. "You can break your neck on these things." The arm that used to hang on Rachel swings lifeless by his side, the fingers dancing. He is a man among no men. As he rises up the stairs—head tightening, ears burning, sweat dripping salty into his eyes, heart jumping as if into an abyss—he can feel his body again. The humid air grows colder, the clouds gathering—he *knew* it was January!—and underneath the silence, underneath the static, Abe hears a rumble. He's getting closer.

Finally he reaches the top of the stairs and sees the men gathering outside of the synagogue. He cries, "Elza!" It comes out like a croak, airless, watery.

The men of Tarnów, the men of Venice, the men of Jerusalem turn to face him.

"Elza," he determines.

But instead a middle-aged man separates from the human clump outside of the synagogue and walks over to him. Abe holds his breath. *They might still be here. What if they shoot this man for disobeying orders?*

No gunshot. This man has dark skin and sunburned green eyes. His face is encircled by rough, blazing, black, curly hair fraying gray at the temples. "Elza," Abe murmurs as the man approaches. Before Abe can protest—*he is just a little boy, after all*—the man places a light hand on his shoulder.

"Are you all right, my brother?" the man asks.

"My sister," Abe screeches. "She took her."

"Who took her?"

"They pulled her out into the street. She died in the street!" Tears fall from Abe's eyes.

The man averts his gaze. *Why won't he look at me? Is he working together with Rachel?* Abe takes a closer look. The man's hair falls over his face like a dark curtain. *Rachel.*

She's always one step ahead of you. Even when you went back to Venice after the war—after the war? But it's still only—even then, remember? You wanted to take her into that

*synagogue, to show her how you liberated it, but that bitch
overtook you and walked in first. You think it was an accident?
How'd your tea taste today? A little funny?*

"My sister," Abe tries again, composing himself. "I need
to find my sister. Maybe you know her. Her name is Elza."

"Let me take you home, my brother," the man says. He
links his arm with Abe's. "Where do you live?"

Abe shivers. "Not here," he gasps. He can't let this man
take him back to that house. *She might be there.* It isn't his.
His. But before he can think about it, the address slips out
of his mouth. An address spoken in Hebrew. A Jerusalem
address.

"I can take you there," the man says. "That's just on the
next street, down the stairs."

Rachel stands outside the house when they arrive, face pale.

"I'm returning your boy," the man says.

Rachel grabs at the buttons of Abe's shirt, right at the tea
stain. "The gate was closed," she says. "The gate was closed!"

Distracted by their faces, Abe murmurs a reassurance.
Rachel and the man. The dark hair. So unlike his. *Where
are their faces? Why will no one in this neighborhood show their
face? Too similar. And look at how they smile at each other, so
knowingly.*

Musty air pushes in from the walls of homes all around
him. Standing-water air. *There is no space here, in this city.
It's unnatural to live like this, away from cars, from shops, from
culture. You can't let her take you back in there.*

The sagging clouds gather, yet somehow Rachel and the
man's dark hair still burn in the harsh sunlight. He feels it
on his own scalp. It always burned like that when he had
to pause under the desert sun to show his military papers.

Papers. Rachel must have documents somewhere. Things leave a trail. The trail of water behind the ship that delivered him to Venice. He would have to go back into the house and look. *But she would know. Always hovering over him, always lurking.*

He lets her lead him into the house. He lets her lean him against the banister, one hand supporting his weight on the entry table. He lets her sculpt him, mold him, control him, lets her believe he needs her. He knows the layout of this house. He knows his way around it now. He came back after the war. Should have or should not have, he did. He may have lost control there for a few seconds, a few years, but it is his again. His country, his city, his neighborhood, his house. *His.* He just has to play dumb for a few minutes longer.

She links his arm with hers and starts leading him toward the stairs. When they reach the landing, she pauses, looks at him.

"All right?" she asks.

He hums, then releases his arm from hers. He nods. The arm dangles, no longer lifeless, the palm dancing over Rachel's lower back. The marble stairs stretch out before him. The curtain of dark hair covers her face. *It would only take one push.*

IN THE CITY OF THE DEAD

BY ILAI ROWNER

Har HaMenuchot Cemetery

1

They hailed a cab to Jerusalem outside of the airport and ogled the traffic from the backseat. Cars flew down the road, which was surrounded by fields. In the distance, David saw a tractor and a plow. Things happened here too. The view kept changing in front of their eyes. How would they know where the road went, which direction they were going? All of a sudden, doubt sprouted in Joseph's mind: *Will the road lead us where we want to go?* The question echoed inside of him. *Wherever we go, that is where this road leads.* He cleared his throat, wiped his nose, and turned to face the taxi driver.

"Where are you taking us?" he asked. "Where do we go from here? Where are you headed?"

The driver glanced uncomfortably in the rearview mirror. "Jerusalem. You asked to go to Jerusalem." Then he added, "I go where you tell me."

"But where in Jerusalem?" David asked, thinking, *The road leads knowledge to its place. But we've never been here before.* If knowledge didn't know where it was going, the road would twist and fade into places they'd never been.

"Where in Jerusalem do you want to go?" the driver asked, startling them from their reveries.

They didn't know what to say. What even was there in

Jerusalem? Where did they need to go? Where did the road lead to? They recalled the photograph on the wall of the Parisian Jew's delicatessen: the Old City and the golden dome among the walls. David remembered the name of the desert town from the works of different authors, back when he was young and still read books. Glassy-eyed and gape-mouthed, he reminisced about ancient stones and ruins: Jerusalem and Athens (and possibly Rome too), the cradles of Western civilization, from the days when he still traveled abroad, like other tourists.

"Tell me, Joseph," he said, looking at his fellow traveler with suspicion, "what are we doing here? What did we come for?" All of a sudden, a deceptive vision of decent people ran through him. Ha ha, a deceptive vision of decent people who always know where they are going and what they have to look forward to: enjoying the good life at a hotel, standing around a church or museum, watching the desolate desert from a lookout point designed for scholars. *This is the period of Enlightenment, my friends, the cradle of civilization in Jerusalem. This is where peoples and nations passed through, leaving their mark before they went extinct, this is where time faces history.*

The car slowed down. A man was standing tall on the shoulder of the road, pointing right and left, up and down, probably looking for something, or perhaps guarding something. David and Joseph watched him from the window. Joseph sighed. David pictured the bald man as a kind of Roman senator in a white gown, or a bearded Roman governor, some sort of Pontius Pilate rebuking him at the gate, pointing an accusing finger at him: *Barbarian! Who are you and what are you doing here?*

Joseph pulled a piece of paper from his pocket (he felt the pride of the elder, the power of responsibility), a small note the Jew had given them in case they got lost on their way. The note bore a clear address: *Har HaMenuchot Cemetery*. An indecipherable map was drawn beneath the address, leading them to the city entrance, the city's edge, the city of the dead in Jerusalem.

Joseph passed the note to the driver, who slipped his glasses over his nose.

"Straight from the airport to a funeral," the man said. "Unlucky. This is no place to stay the night or leave your suitcases. This is not a cheap boardinghouse or a hotel with a view of the mountains."

"We have no suitcases," said David. "We came with nothing. We don't even have a change of clothes."

"But you've got cab fare," the driver smiled.

David was fisting the handle of a briefcase packed with money that rested on his lap. "A funeral? We are just agents, agents from Paris."

"Here on business?"

David stuttered, then got his bearings: "We are managers, inspectors from Paris. We're here on business, yes."

The driver nodded. "Well, as long as you have petty cash to pay for this ride."

Now Joseph turned David's face toward him and grabbed him by the knee. Wordlessly, he told him, *Shut up! Don't you dare say another word.*

The two of them remained tight-lipped until the taxi veered off the main road and into the city at Saharov Gardens.

2

They paused at the center of the cemetery and took in the view. It was a frigid morning hour and the mountains rose up all around them, green and rocky. The air was saturated with dew and dark, pregnant clouds slid downward, kissing the earth, trembling between the valleys. Joseph stared silently. David lowered his head and listened to the sound of his own footsteps.

"I've never seen this many graves in my life," he heard himself say. Alleys of dead. Levels of burial plots; flat, exposed gravestones. The field of corpses stretched all the way to the cliff, rectangles upon rectangles, uniform and anonymous, covering the nearby hills like herds of cattle. Here and there he saw visitors, gathered families or individuals in winter religious hats. Prayer canopies flapped in the wind, and in the distance cars carried the bodies, laid out in multipurpose wooden coffins, while all around a crowd swayed, a swarm of people descending from the hill, like a picture.

"What are we doing here?" David said, looking up.

"Are you asking *me*?"

"I . . ."

They stood, surrounded by rows, a procession of gravestones.

Joseph looked away with contempt. "Can you imagine?"

"What's there to imagine?"

"All the bones underneath us."

David read out the names to his right: "Sheindel and Ora Binyamin, mother and daughter." Then to his left: "Yitzhak Ben Naftali, may he rest in peace. All of these people?"

"Bones talk," said Joseph. Ha ha. "Can you hear them?" Then he murmured, "Life makes a hell of a lot of noise, but what remains?"

"A long silence," said David. "One long silence."

The wind caressed their faces.

They were alone.

"Listen," Joseph prompted. Then: "Listen, it's ongoing . . . it's unending."

"That's why they bind them with rock and stone, huh?"

"Separated with stone plaques."

"The dead?"

"To keep them from interfering with the general silence."

"Yes, yes."

"Ever tried picking up a gravestone?"

David said nothing.

"Ever lie underneath the rock and listen?"

"What could you possibly hear?"

"The bones rattling. The heart beating in the darkness."

"That's frightening," David mumbled.

3

They spent a long time walking among the graves, through the pathways of plots, descending the short asphalt road, circling the hill from the west and climbing up the other way. Here they passed through the Sephardic and Mizrahi kabbalah scholars' plot, there they visited the Breslov Chassid plot, attempting to decipher markers and signposts. Jerusalem pine trees swelled above them in the northern wind, and they felt as if they were treading the paths of some bizarre zoo. But here, the animals, the monkeys and bears were bare rocks, gravestones, compartments sealed by high walls. They discovered family portraits painted on a red marble wall, the graves of rabbis or forgotten saints, medicine men and mystics, and beatified folks (some more and some less), their names appearing in Cyrillic lettering in French, English, and Hebrew. Nearby, open graves were filled with broken glass and cement, empty plastic bottles strewn where flesh and bone once rotted, now transformed into a neglected heap of refuse. At the end of the row were the tiny stone plaques of children who never grew up.

David panted and wheezed. "Rest!" he cried, gesturing toward a bench.

They sat, the briefcase by David's side. Fortunately, they had stuffed themselves with as much food as they could (bread rolls, omelets, yogurt) during their night flight from Paris. Their stomachs did not bother them. They were no longer hungry. It was quiet again. They spent long moments staring at the expanse, their eyes dancing between the few passersby before hanging in midair, their focus dulling.

David's voice rose casually, as if he'd just opened his mouth to yawn and a question slipped out: "What are we doing here?"

Joseph said nothing.

"Do you remember?"

"I don't feel like remembering."

"It should have come to us easily, what the thing is."

"Are you sure?"

"We didn't just come here for no reason at all," David insisted.

"True."

"How odd."

"I don't remember much."

"How about now?" asked David.

"What about now?"

"We're here."

"It's over now. Look at how we're dressed—like relatives." Joseph sighed.

"And they gave us the briefcase . . ."

"This is a job for professionals."

"They'll think we had something to do with it!"

"How do you mean?"

"With the ousting."

"Of the leader? Of Isaac?"

"With Isaac's ousting."

"So you *do* know what we're doing here?"

"Stop playing dumb."

"Are you hearing yourself?"

"I didn't cajole the boss. I didn't oust or murder. How about you?"

"I only murdered my wife. I've stayed out of it ever since."

4

"Your wife?" David marveled. "I had no idea." After a brief pause, he asked, "Did you serve time for it? How long?"

Joseph didn't answer. Then he asked, "How much do you know?"

"Not much," David evaded. "Nothing, really. I know nothing about you."

In a near whisper, Joseph said, "I don't remember much, either."

"About your wife?"

"I hardly remember a thing. A thing! In fact, I remember nothing. Only that she was strangled to death one day and I was accused of murdering her."

They sat in silence.

As if to himself, David repeated, "Strangled to death one day."

"Because I became involved in the thieving business," Joseph suddenly offered.

"You?"

"I kept myself busy stealing all night. I was addicted."

"To the money?"

"To the revolving-door roulette."

David stared blankly.

"I was addicted to the feeling of breaking into a stranger's home," Joseph explained, looking at David. "The door revolves and you're inside. And then . . ." He gesticulated his words into life: "You walk down a dark hallway. The rooms are empty. The first few times, my legs shook, my knees buckled. Sometimes I used a small flashlight, a face covering . . . The door revolves and you know it's out of your hands—life, I mean. Fate. Whatever you want to call it. In a minute, you'll either get caught or you'll grab your treasure." Then he added, "I kept knives at home just in case."

"What?"

"I'd sharpen knives at home so I could have them ready if I needed to stab somebody before fleeing with the loot."

"And did you ever stab anyone?"

"One time they shot at us. They took us by surprise, hiding behind the sofa. My knives were no good then." Joseph glanced up and blew his nose. "I remember the color of the sofa. They took us by surprise. I'll never forget it."

"In the dark?"

"There was a lamp on. I remember the face of some old bag, this flawed specimen, this clumsy cow. All of a sudden she popped her head out and shot at us."

"Were you injured, ha ha?"

"I held onto my shoulder on the way out of there. That lady shot me, ha ha, we escaped out the back like a couple of criminals."

"Which you were."

"Criminals?"

"Yes."

"Robbers!"

"What's the difference?"

"I barely made it out of there alive. Maybe that's why she suffocated."

"Suffocated?"

Joseph paused. "Maybe that's why my wife . . . I mean, my wife was strangled. She wet her pants. One day she was deader than dead."

"They shot at you and your wife is the one who died?"

"It isn't inconceivable."

"You think?"

"I think it's conceivable."

"Then why are you smiling like that?" David asked.

"How?"

"Like that, like that. Like you're smiling right now. You have a vicious smile on your face."

"She wanted me to quit, you know . . . we argued about it. I was addicted to break-ins . . . it turned into a big argument, then hatred in her eyes. She threatened me, so I gave it to her straight."

David struggled to refocus his eyes. "How many years did you serve for that?"

Joseph's vicious smile persisted. "Why do you think I agreed to come with you?" he insinuated.

"I don't get it," said the bespectacled beggar.

"You're too nice, David! There's a lot you don't get!"

5

"Listen," Joseph said, his voice thicker.

David nodded.

"Why'd you think I came here? To find a burial plot for the boss?"

They breathed.

"To find Mr. Kiegel his cave for the afterlife?"

"Why, then?" David asked defensively.

"Can't you see?"

David shrugged.

"Can't you see? The boss was murdered or ousted or removed from his post, and for whom? For the family. And the Jews sent us to find him a burial plot . . . Do you see what I'm getting at?"

"I'm trying to."

"It is a good opportunity to run, David." Joseph fixed his eyes on the briefcase full of cash and smiled to himself. "In twenty years I've never had this kind of golden opportunity to wriggle out of those handcuffs. It's over. In twenty years, I've never had this kind of opportunity to flee bondage."

David nodded with trepidation, not fully understanding. "What changed? What, um, changed all of a sudden?"

"I've been asleep for twenty years and now I'm waking up from a bad dream. That's why I was closed off like that on the airplane. I just shut my eyes and fell asleep." He looked into David's eyes.

He seemed different to David. For the first time, David feared Joseph.

"The boss is dead," Joseph announced. "He left us. What's going to happen to Sammy and Miriam and Ronny? The family's freaking out. What are you going to do without him? You know, as far as I'm concerned, they can all go . . . And why'd they send us here with this money? Huh, David? You and I, of all people. Two aging, uneducated chauffeurs. Why'd they send us? To get rid of us just in time, so that we couldn't listen in on all their trouble before they elect a new head for their tribe."

"Over there, look at them," David cried out, as if suddenly remembering. He pointed at gardeners working among

the graves, between heaven and earth. They were digging a
hole on the edge of the plot. The agents watched: the field
of corpses stretched over to the slope, and the two laborers
dissolved into small black silhouettes.

"We'll ask them where the tycoons' offices are," David
said. "We've got to get rid of the briefcase." Then he added,
"We have to pay a deposit to secure a spot."

"How much money do you think is in there?" Joseph
asked, looking at the briefcase again.

"Thousands, for sure."

"How can you tell?"

"Weight. There's a handsome pile in there."

Joseph snorted with satisfaction and spit to his side.

"For starters, I think it's a round number."

"For sure," Joseph said.

"A round number in international currency."

"And that's only the beginning. Imagine."

"That's for certain."

"These people buy their burial plots with gold bars," Joseph said. "Anything to guarantee they can be buried in holy
dirt, in case the messiah ever shows up. The whole thing
reeks—as in, stinks—if you ask me. Why would they murder
the boss? One of their own? Why would they murder their
own big shot and then do good in the eyes of God, funding a
special flight in a coffin for the guy and a cemetery up on the
mountain?"

"Listen—"

"And why were we, two brainiacs like ourselves, sent all
the way over here to find a burial plot for the leader in the
city of Jerusalem?"

"These Jews know what they're doing. They have a
promise."

"A promise?"

"From God. Go figure."

"The whole thing sounds made up. Fiction."

"Are you listening?"

Joseph gave the briefcase a sidelong glance. "I don't think we should."

"Should what?"

"Give it up like that. What'd we come all this way for?"

"What are you saying?"

"I'm saying I'd get on the horse right now and flee east." Joseph peered up at the sky and pointed like Napoleon signaling toward the Alps. "East."

"Where to?"

"Persia, India. Through the desert. I'd take the money and run, no doubt. Give me the briefcase." Joseph's voice changed, his words stabbing: "Let me count the money in the briefcase."

"The bills, you mean?"

"Let me see those wads. Want to?" Joseph's smile was peculiar.

"Leave it."

But Joseph had already pounced on the briefcase like a fox on a chicken.

"Leave it!" David pushed him away. "If you love Isaac, let him die in peace."

"I did love him."

"I loved him too. I loved the boss more than I loved myself."

"And if he was ousted—"

"He was betrayed!"

"That's what I'm saying. We ought to run."

But David wouldn't meet his eyes. "It's locked, the briefcase. Nowhere to run."

"You've got the key?"

"It's locked, that's what they told me."

"And you don't have the key?"

"God forbid. I've got nothing on me. Go ahead and check."

"They didn't give you the key?"

David shook his head and pulled his pockets inside out. "I've got nothing." Then he mumbled mindlessly, "I've got nothing in my pockets, you can check if you want."

"Are you sure? Then how are we supposed to open it?"

"We won't open it. We'll do what we were sent here to do. We'll go pay at the office."

Joseph shifted restlessly. "They didn't trust you, Mr. Clumsy? Your friends didn't trust you enough to give you a key?"

"I don't know."

"No matter," said Joseph. "Let's break the lock with a rock, huh? Give it to me, I'll go find one."

"Are you sure?"

"What do you mean? We have to make sure there's money in there. We don't want them laughing at us."

"The moneybags at the office. You think they might laugh."

"Yes, if we hand them a briefcase full of gravel."

"You've got nothing to worry about," David now remembered. "Only one person has the key. That's what Sammy told me when we left headquarters."

"What did Sammy tell you?"

"That only one person has the key."

"And how do we find this person?"

"He didn't say."

"What do you mean?"

"Plain and simple, I don't know how we find him."

"You're an idiot, David. What were you thinking?" Then Joseph said, "What do we do if we end up handing them a briefcase full of junk?" Again, he tried: "I suggest we crack the lock with a rock, open it, and slip a few gold coins into our pockets."

David fidgeted.

"Because of our boss's insult, we deserve to see what's in there," Joseph reasoned.

"What insult?"

"Don't we deserve a few coins? We don't even have a key."

David hesitated. "And what if he shows up?"

"Who?"

"The man with the key."

"What does he even look like?"

"Like some guy, that's for sure."

"Like what, a gatekeeper with a key?"

"If this key shows up and he sees we broke the briefcase open with—"

"Where would he pop out from?"

"What do you mean?" David asked.

"We don't know what this guy with the key looks like. If he shows up, God forbid, we'll come up with something. We'll say we had no choice. We'll make something up. We'll come up with something about a lack of choice."

"That's convincing. It's convincing, Joseph."

"We'll say we're just borrowing, not stealing. That makes a world of difference. We're just borrowing a few bucks, for a limited time. It's just a different perspective."

David gawked at him.

"An unabsolute perception of reality. Just borrowing for a little while. Nothing has to be set in stone like it is in reality."

"I'm afraid," David admitted.

"What's the worst that could happen?"

"Can't you tell?"

"We'll slip it into our pockets, take on a few IOUs. Call it whatever you like, and let's hit the road." Joseph paused. "A miracle happened to us, David. We've been stuck in crime for twenty years. Twenty years in servitude to our master. Look around you. Who knows us here? What are we supposed to do in Jerusalem?" He was getting heated. "This cemetery, it's a serious affair for the dead. They're waiting in line to become worm food. But what about those of us who want to live? What if we're still not finished polluting the planet with our excretions, huh?"

6

But David still wasn't convinced. "And what if Isaac comes and can't find his hole? Can't you see what might happen?"

"What might happen?"

"It'll end badly. We won't keep our promise."

"Our promise?"

"The promise we made to the family. On Judgment Day, the Resurrection, what do I know . . ." In a different voice, David said, "You've heard the story about the patricide."

"Which one? There are many."

"Many fathers?"

"Many stories."

"And many murdering sons."

"Ha ha."

"But this is one story," David clarified. "A logical story from the Middle Ages."

"And you believe it?"

"I don't know what I believe." David wiped his mouth brusquely. "Do you?"

Joseph said nothing.

"Now listen to the story," David said. "Once upon a time there was a king."

"Ooh la la," Joseph grunted. "That does sound familiar."

"I told you," said David. "The good king blessed his sons and daughters, when all of a sudden one son stood up, drew his sword, and stabbed the king in the heart."

"Just like that? Suddenly?"

"All of a sudden."

"And you really believe that makes sense?"

"It makes sense for the Middle Ages," David said.

"But why did the son murder his father just like that, out of nowhere?" Joseph pressed, his tongue heavy.

"For a few coins, Joseph. Just like you."

"Like me?"

"And not only that!" David thundered, enflamed. "He dragged his father's body outside and dug him a grave! Are you listening? He laid his father in the grave."

"So? What do we care about that?"

"Something else happened," David explained. "When he was almost finished sealing the coffin, a third man came up behind the son and shoved him in there as well." He took a breath.

"Who was that?"

"The third man."

"And he shoved the bloody son in? The murderer?"

"He slammed the king's coffin shut on the guy, you hear? The son tried to push his way out, to haggle, to scream. He yelled, *Let me out! Let me out!*"

"Just like that."

"He banged on the coffin from the inside: *Out! Out!*"

"But he was shoved into his father's coffin?"

"He was crushed, the scoundrel."

"He was trapped in there, the slayer."

"That's what happens to people who don't pay their debts, Joseph. Just like you."

"Like *me?*" the agent protested.

"Crooks are buried alive along with their victims," David concluded. "That's all you need to know."

"So, what, is that the end of the story? The end of the game?"

"This is an end without an end."

"Why?"

"Because who can know the process of rotting . . . Who can know, Joseph, better than you?" said David. "In the end, the greedy man finds nothing, not even his own bones."

ECLIPSE

BY ZOHAR ELMAKIAS

Temple Mount

F irst the architect died. Then the lamb died. Then I died.

Meaning, first the idea of a city died. Then the concept of a future died. Then I died.

But first things first—here's what happened: Just before last summer, I got a call from a professor who teaches at the American university I attended as a research student a few years back. I'd participated in two of her seminars; we had formed a kind of animosity, the flip side of which is necessarily a potential intimacy, but we'd never worked together. She grew up in the Balkans, had seen a rifle or two with her own two eyes, and had once told a small crowd of students that had gathered around her at an overly well-mannered department event: "Violence activates me. I grew up in violence. I feel comfortable with violence." When the event was over and undergrads tucked half-full bottles of white wine in their tote bags, a classmate walked over, quoted that statement about violence, and added with affected pity, "You're the only one who nodded when she said that."

I must have nodded so hard that now I once again found myself on the coast of the Mediterranean, up to my elbows in violence, on the phone with that professor. She had to settle a few open questions related to her forthcoming book about Jerusalem, she'd said. Or maybe she said she had to lay the foundations. And she remembered me, that I was from there. She imagined the project would operate like a mole: she had no eyes because she was far away, but she had me, so near, as her nose. Most importantly, like a mole, the whole thing had to be done underground, with no surface presence. As many hallways, burrows, and tunnels as possible. As little as possible of the Western Wall Plaza, the sanitizing light of the sun.

My first task was to interview the former city architect. I lied about the nature of the project, all nice and polite via email, and arrived at our meeting well-packed and put-together with a list of accurately phrased questions I'd sent him in advance. I sat with my back to the wall, a mighty desk separating us. He no longer does urban projects. He had switched to country-style housing, only private homes between the river and the sea, garden deck upon garden deck of fine wood, endless balconies hanging over agricultural terraces, olive trees, an arid Tuscany. Still, he was happy to say a word or two about his old life, about a city that had been cobbled together, which, to a great extent, he'd designed, forging it from bedrock, birthing it from the seam. We spoke for three hours or so about how the city was built, about why he'd made this or that decision at the time, about what the mountain might be concealing (*the* mountain—the Temple Mount), about archeological expeditions, about the Foundation Stone, about winged beasts and the status quo. We went over all the technical details as well as deeper issues, and I checked off question after question in my little brown notebook.

When I was about to leave he called my name. I half turned toward him, suddenly fully awake.

"You won't learn a thing from what I've told you," he said. "The lock that is Jerusalem has a single key: Figure out the mountain on foot. You should ascend it at least three times. The spirit of the place," he added, "cannot be understood through any tool but the feet." Who are we, if not bodies aroused with spirit by topography? What was topography if not desolation given a body? His architectural theory came with halachic decrees: no leather shoes, in a state of purity, having dipped in the mikvah the previous night. He was secular, he clarified. Utterly secular. But out in public, we'd best all be orthodox.

I went out into the dark and chilly stairwell, looked down at the beige terrazzo floors, thought about the eighties, then about the future, and then about the architect. I felt nauseated. My ribs flinched and my shoulders jerked forward. I grabbed my stomach with both hands, my neck curved with shocking snakiness. The seizure repeated itself once, twice, three times. Then my body relinquished control to me and I reached out to the banister, stumbled down three or four floors on light, shaky legs, my stomach like a fish tank carried by metal arms, watery. I walked out into the sun-scorched street. In the white expanse that flooded my field of vision, I imagined seeing a twisting line on the horizon, a snake that had swallowed an elephant. No, a mountain.

Upon my return to my home between the Carmel Market and the sea, I drafted a brief and polite email to the professor, attaching a recording of my conversation with the architect, as well as a document into which I'd typed up my notes from the brown notebook. *We are formulating a relationship,* I thought. *I need a job. It's important to show her I can do it; it would be in my best interest to show up.* I could see the Hassan Bek Mosque from my window. I found myself hypnotized by the green light, my fingers lingered. I added a quick line about ascending the mountain: *I know you didn't ask me to do that, but it seems important. I'll do it in my free time and send updates shortly.*

The professor responded that same night with uncharacteristic enthusiasm, instructing me to bill her for the mountain hours, trying to create a sameness, a similarity between us, asking me not to skip a single detail, to tell her everything, as if she were up there with me, riding on my back. The gap between us was already gnawing.

That was on Thursday. I spent most of the weekend lying on the living room floor, trying to cool off. On Friday night, I went out. Everything drew away from me. (Friends nodded when I told them about my visit to Jerusalem, the one I'd made, the one I was planning to make; one said, "That guy sounds insane.")

On Monday, I had already ascended the mountain. I say "ascended" as if it were one thing, a single, swift motion, a sword slicing through flesh with one fell swoop, but in fact several things happened in succession. What they all had in common was upward movement, soaring. The bus to Jerusalem stood in traffic, as usual. As always before entering the city, I had the kind of stomachache people have before they visit the dentist. I leaned my head against the window, knowing a red heat spot would remain on my forehead for a spell. I squeezed my eyes shut. I walked along the light rail route from the Central Bus Station to the Mughrabi Gate outside the Old City, waiting first in the Jewish line, then in the tourist line. I didn't want a police escort. Everything was supposed to be totally underground. A curious French family waited ahead of me, and a band of musicians in white suddenly sidled up to the line to sing to an American bar mitzvah boy who was standing in a clump with his parents and some aunts, smiling and flushed. The police officer half smiled at me, signaling exhaustedly for me to pass through. She didn't even ask me anything. She could see it all on me. I walked slowly up the shaky ramp, attentive, trembling, trying to pay attention. To my right was the new model of the Jewish temple, contained inside a large glass case. Above it were the words: *Peacefully, respectfully, and in awe, as one walks through a king's palace, one's home.*

Every single thing in this city gets turned into a maquette, one on top of the other. I recalled the model of nineteenth-century Jerusalem ensconced in one of the lower, darker rooms of the Tower of David, a sort of enormous relief made diligently by a Hungarian bookbinder. I once slipped my fingers between its buildings when no one was looking, so beautiful, as if the stones were glued together by tweezers, and each stone—the divine essence of Jerusalem. The real city could never compete with a model, I thought. We are expected to ascend to the real city under the burning sun, like hot air floating upward, while this concealed, perfect Jerusalem is descended into through cool stones, in a darkening space, down, down, down.

Beside the temple model was a small group of Israelis with a smiling police officer who patiently and decisively explained the rules. For a moment they seemed like a family, and the police officer was the forgiving, disciplinarian mother. I lingered, half listening (for the professor's sake, I reminded myself). "What we're trying to maintain here," the officer said, "isn't just the security thing, but also local customs. We want to keep everything as respectful and positive as possible. We respect everybody, no incidents, so that the tourists can keep coming. As far as you're concerned, we have to make sure you're wearing modest clothing, of course, without too many exterior symbols or whatnot, no alcohol because this is a holy place after all and we respect it, no weapons obviously, that goes without saying, even *we* don't carry any around here. And one last thing, my friends—we don't enter the mosque. The Waqf officers out front ask questions in order to make sure they only let in Muslims, so please don't mess with them. We follow protocol for now, until the messiah comes," she laughed, "keeping the place as welcoming and touristy as possible."

When I reached the top, I walked out through the Chain Gate. Two girls in military uniforms and high, tight ponytails stared at me casually, watching my heat-flushed face and then my back as I moved back into the beating of busy streets, a member of the flock once more. I took the route that, over the next few months, would become a sort of prayer route when I ascended the mountain again and again as if possessed. I memorized the way like it was a psalm, always in the early morning, always with my eyes lowered. Jewish Quarter Street, Perfume Market Street, Oil Mill Street, Hakimronim, Haguy, Via Dolorosa. I would press the guesthouse buzzer, open the gate, climb the stairs, Via Dolorosa, I'd walk past religious symbols, something moving within me, stirring my emotions, I'd walk out through the old cafeteria, burgundy velvet all around, first to the large balcony, the monstrous cacti, then up to the roof. I spun on an axis over and over again, looking at the city roofs, then back at the golden dome.

That first time I was up on the mountain, I felt nothing at all. There were layers upon layers of nothing between me and the mountain. I was completely guarded: the backpack, the hat, the sunglasses. I was almost disappointed. I expected I'd have something to tell the professor, about the mountain itself, not only the entrance and the prep. Everything I had to tell her now was easy information, I'd discovered nothing new. And if I'd learned nothing, I hoped to feel something at least, to make some kind of return, to imagine some sort of home, to grow sick with the sudden spirit that invaded me, to be struck by the blindness of faith. Instead there were neither advances in knowledge nor in feeling.

When I was in the middle of the roof, my stupid phone rang. The screen flashed lime-green, no caller ID. One ring, two rings, three. I picked up midring, to take them by surprise. It was the architect's wife. We hadn't met. She only said, "This is the architect's wife," and I knew. She said she'd found my phone number on that enormous desk, written in pencil on a cardboard archive folder, along with my name. "I think he left some sketches here for you," she said. "Archaic-looking ones."

"Left?" I asked in a near whisper.

"Left," she said. "He went out on Friday and we're not sure where he is. I went into his study to look for a datebook, but instead I found this folder, so I figured I'd call."

"I'll come get it," I said, shading my eyes needlessly, I had so many protective layers on. "Can I come by later?"

She confirmed softly. We hung up.

Then I realized that I had lain down on the roof toward the end of the conversation, unsure why. The floor rubbed against my elbow, and the bunned hair massaged the back of my neck. I was exhausted.

By the time I opened my eyes again, the sun had set, yet the humidity still hung heavily in the air. My phone had died. I made my way to Jaffa Gate, then out to the light rail. I boarded without a ticket and held onto a pole, almost leaning. I glanced at the smart phone of a young man sitting below me. He kept refreshing a news site's home page, probably waiting for the results of a soccer match. The red logo stretched down slowly, then jumped back up. One of the small captions summarized: *Former City Architect Found Dead in a Natural Spring in the Jerusalem Mountains*.

I felt dizzy. I no longer had the courage to go near that house. I rushed back to my coastal town.

"What a coincidence," the professor's image said on my computer screen that night, "water and mountain." She seemed to care only about the literary aspect of it all, not about the folder or the phone call. She was almost bored. She jotted down everything I remembered from the police officer's speech, enjoying the shorthand.

Toward the end of the conversation, I tried to tell her that I'd go pick up those sketches sometime soon, but she was already distracted. "I'm going away next week to get some rest and write the introduction to the book," she said. "I'll call you from there, from a landline."

I counted seven days exactly, then emailed a few words of comfort and a request to the architect's inbox, which seemed like it might be shared by him and his wife, and collapsed into a fretful sleep. At dawn, a truck honked outside my window. Eyes wide open, I dragged myself over to the computer. My inbox contained seven files, photographed sloppily by a cell phone's camera. I was familiar with most of the images— rough maps, archeological cross sections, a shabby sketch of Jerusalem on the Madaba Map. But the last file contained two images I'd never seen before: a two-page spread from a research book, on the corner of which the architect had written *Monk* in thick pencil. Each page featured a near square with a map of Jerusalem. On the left page, Jerusalem was transposed over a topographic image, like an enormous and complex fingerprint, with a caption that read: *Gordon's map of Jerusalem, showing the figure of Christ in the contour intervals of the terrain.* The right page featured a much simpler map, four or five thin lines composing a shape topped by a cross, with a tiny headlike form atop the cross, along with the word *Golgotha.* The caption read, *Gordon's sketch of the human figure superimposed upon the map of Jerusalem.* I was only vaguely familiar with modern attempts to place Golgotha and with traditions comparing the shape of Jerusalem to the human form, as if it was not only the heart of the world, but an actual physical heart. I couldn't figure out what the architect was trying to tell me. I stared at the maps until my eyes burned. On the edges of the right map I suddenly noticed another form, something reminiscent of an anthill, a mold stain, or a tunnel, as if marked by powder. In the heart of the wormlike shape I read, in English, the words *Mount of Olives*.

Then the lamb died.

The second task the professor gave me, in a broken phone call from her summer house on the West Coast, was to document a ritual sacrifice. The timing was perfect. I made two phone calls, and nine days later I was already temporarily attached to a group of tourists who had come to donate a shekel or two for the cause of the Third Temple. Their hosts put on a whole show for them. We were standing on the Mount of Olives, our backs to the camels draped with red rugs, carriers of tourism, facing the golden dome, countless graves stretching under our chins. It was only May and already sweltering, and the lamb was curled up in a plastic pail on the ground, right by the railing. Someone said they'd bought a five-thousand-shekel butcher's knife at a home goods store in Mamila and that it was on its way over by taxi. Since the Jews didn't have a temple yet, only a gentile was allowed to perform the ritual, the rabbi explained once I'd introduced myself. "So we're just playing here, but we're like kids—we play very seriously."

He sent a Palestinian laborer who happened to walk by to grab a rock or two, and a whisper ran through the small crowd, growing into a cracked cry. Our gentile had overslept.

A man in dirty white linen stepped forward, his hands together in a prayer shape in front of his chest, and said, "I'm a gentile, and a butcher too."

I thought, *There is no man that has not his hour.*

The new gentile removed his shoes and swayed back and forth, mumbling to himself, as if in encouragement. Then he picked up the lamb and caressed him (yes, caressed him), and spoke of the fire of God, of shame, of the earth being a whore, of his hands soon to be stained with blood. Behind us, a procession of coughing speakers sounded, *Oseh shalom bimromav,* and all that, and a class of bar and bat mitzvah kids followed the noise, white and blue and silver balloons trailing above them.

I tried to understand something about symbols (knife, lamb, rock), but failed. Instead I thought about everyday matters (camels, balloons, taxis). I tried to dedicate my gaze to the lamb. The architect had commanded me to look, and so did my conscience. There were more cameras than people between me and the lamb, and yet I watched very, very hard, thinking, *There, just like the architect, now the lamb's going to die.* The blood was bright, almost orange, not exactly real.

I watched intently, but its sullied eye remained sealed shut. *There is no thing that has not its place.*

On the walk back to the Dung Gate through Hakohanim Way, I looked at my feet, trying to let the sun burn the back of my neck as much as possible, leaving my eyes under the shadow of my hat, keeping my horizon narrow, going blind. The rabbi slowly moved up to the front of the line, lingering next to me for a moment to ask, "So, is there going to be a temple?"

Eyes on the ground, I said, "Who knows."

There was utter silence, and a pause, the kind that happens when you come up with a new idea.

I stopped and looked up.

He met my eyes with a clear gaze and said, "Everybody knows."

Back home, I called the professor. She picked up but kept her camera off the whole time. I spoke enthusiastically to the gray square that displayed her name, gesticulating, describing the sacrifice with utter devotion, saying even the things that sounded deranged. I wanted all of it, everything I'd seen, to be hers. As I spoke, my eyes wandered to the square where I appeared. I noticed the fresh tan line across my forehead, the pale skin that had been previously covered by the hat, the hair sticky with sweat. There was a black smear above my right eyebrow, dirt and congealed blood under my fingernails. I'd forgotten I'd touched things. That things had touched me. I'd forgotten I'd watched an animal turn into meat, that I'd let meat be a thing that touched me, a thing I lived alongside of. I hadn't eaten a bite of it—it was forbidden. What had happened was much worse: the sacrifice had entered my body through the epidermis. I think the professor noticed it too. I could hear it in her voice. The nodding attentiveness of the first few minutes of conversation dwindled into a long "Mm-hmm" that contained a question mark.

"I think that's enough for now," she finally said. "I think you should get some rest." Then she added something about budgets, something about nonfiction, how we might want to approach it from a different angle, not sure how academic any of this was, it was unnecessary as research at the moment.

I ended the call winded, suddenly limp, like a parachute that had fallen to the ground. I knew I wouldn't be speaking to her again. The third task was one I gave myself.

Finally, I died.

I became sick from the light. I think I should have obeyed from the start: only in the dark, only underground. Instead, I just went up and higher.

After my last conversation with the professor, I wandered my own home like a guest, making sure not to leave any trace. In the mornings I looked into the round magnifying mirror that reached toward me on a metal arm from the bathroom wall. My face was exhausted, torn, like the face of a character witnessing something horrendous in a film, but the pupils glowed a constant, generous, all-consuming black. I looked at her, she looked at me. It was as if I was under the influence. One mustn't look into a mirror like that. The mutual gaze transforms into a devouring. We looked at each other, we devoured each other, together, again and again.

I knew I'd go back up. I had no choice. Rosh Hashanah was approaching. I booked a room at the Ein Karem convent. I spent the days sitting at the foot of the open-armed Virgin Mary, so small, or on benches, or on the stone path across from the thickening mountainous landscape, envisioning golden stalactites through the black bars, ancient domes in every direction. I wandered the paths of small gardens, looked at the graves of children with a morose expression, leaned against cool stone walls for long moments, breathed inside every space. At night, I lay on the thin mattress, buried books inside the nook in the wall (I didn't care about the contents, only about the material, the paper), along with my phone, no charger, letting it slowly die.

One morning, an older nun asked where I was from. We spoke a little, attentively and hesitantly. She had old words, it was like speaking to the origins of Hebrew. I'm not sure what I was trying to become there, then; what I was trying to mimic in spirit or in flesh. The days at Ein Karem were suspended. I barely left the convent gates and yet my soul stormed. I barely ate during those days, only bread from the corner store and olive oil, only very early in the morning, and then long fasts of perseverance until the next dawn.

I headed out before sunrise on Rosh Hashanah Eve. The mountain opens at seven o'clock during summer months, and I walked out of the convent gates at five. I expected the sun to intensify, but instead it seemed as if behind a blue slide, resembling an old photograph of the sun. I lingered at the Western Wall Plaza, hesitating for just a moment. An older woman pulled me by the arm. I fished some coins from my pocket, and she quickly wrapped a red string around my wrist (when I was younger the strings used to be thinner, and the red had been pure scarlet, not so glowing). After that I seemed to have no choice. I had to cling to the wall, forehead rubbing against the rock, white dust. I tried to hold onto science, what plants are those, memorize and focus, here's a caper bush hanging like a canopy over me, there's a golden henbane. All of a sudden the sun hit me, I lost my balance. As I fell to the ground, I still managed to grab onto the flowers and pull out a few stems. I'm well familiar with fainting, I always faint. Nobody noticed. I managed to fall into a leaning position. As I got up, I twisted the stems into a small bundle and slipped it into my pocket. I walked through the mountain gates into a relatively small crowd. They let us through in groups, introductions made without eye contact but half shouted over hats that covered heads upon heads. At the top, I was gripped with a new urge, not to move closer, but as far as possible, to cling to the outer routes. I recalled what the professor had tried to teach me: to watch, only to watch, to stay close to the walls, as if I were a plant.

I circled the mountain again and again. I spotted things at the edge of my vision. Lips forcefully mumbling prayers behind the backs of police officers; two children playing with a large, tattered foam ball across the plaza; an old woman sitting on a plastic stool and cleaning fava beans, her granddaughter digging through the pile of skins. The sky grayed slowly; first came the chirping of crickets. I heard them behind me and thought I was imagining it, that they were just flashes from my nights in the convent, but they were really there, the chirping growing louder. I saw the old lady turning her head this way and that. On the large, tiled plaza I saw the sudden shadows of birds in flight. I looked up. Enormous flocks were crossing the sky, and the sky was no longer so far away. It was a thick layer of air, so close, as if it had fallen toward us. The children stopped playing when they heard the wild beating of wings whose rhythm changed constantly. The lips of worshippers kept moving, and now I heard a young boy telling his friend, "Do not be terrified by signs in the heavens, though the nations are terrified by them." The passage moved from one mouth to the next, from one person to the next.

And yet the sky continued to darken, and all at once three, four, ten jackals raced onto the path that flanked the mountain, their howling circling around us. The moon grew nearer, closing the distance, and the sun was blocked. I knew this, and yet I peered up at the burning ring in the sky, staring at it until the edges of my vision were colored black, and when I turned to look around the mountain again, I saw people gathering bags that had fallen in confusion and hush, parents reaching out to cover their children's eyes, police officers running, weapons drawn, as if the heavenly bodies were subjected to sovereignty, and platoons in oversized helmets and armor storming from the Chain Gate. I saw the praying boy ducking down at the base of an olive tree. I blinked, confused, here is a great fire, here everything is painted a mustard smog, the tumult of death. I shoved my hand into my pocket, then into my mouth, the golden henbane clinging to the roof of my mouth; a haze fell upon me.

PART III

STONES

ARSON

BY ILAN RUBIN FIELDS

French Hill

P eace Park was on fire. By the time Chief Moshe Lozovsky showed up, all that remained of the trees that
flanked the garden were charred stumps. The flames
had melted the plastic off the jungle gym up until the fire-
fighters turned their hoses on it. A stench that Lozovsky was
familiar with from previous incidents in the Me'ah Shearim
and Shu'afat neighborhoods kept curious onlookers away. A
week later, when he watched the security footage, he'd remember how he thought he'd be finished on French Hill in
a matter of hours.

The park's name was so ironic that no one even bothered
to joke about it. It overlooked the homes of the Palestinian
town of Anata that had sprouted up on the other side of the
wall. Before the fire, there was a climbing structure for children made of a combination of metal and plastic, a circle of
swings, and a large lawn, as well as several benches and water
fountains. Across the way, in Anata, were half-finished buildings with black barrels collecting water on the roofs. There
was no peace, and now there was no park, either. Darkness
descended and the streetlights did not go on.

"Should we go?" Cathy asked.

Lozovsky nodded. "Let's go."

He waited for a report from the fire department to confirm

it was arson, and debated whether or not to go through the trouble of checking the cameras that were always aimed at the walls—perhaps they'd caught something. There were no casualties, and the police had no leads, so there was no reason to investigate any further. Six days later, when he finally spotted a suspect in the security footage, that word—*reason*—would pop back into his mind. He wanted to believe there was a reason someone would set fire to the park, a reason someone would investigate the arson, a reason to arrest the person who had done it, a reason to try him and lock him up. But even if the security footage offered evidence, there was no real reason to make the effort. No true reason; no reason that would be acceptable to this city. In Jerusalem, fires happen because Jerusalemites call for them to happen.

Cathy walked into the room just before he roused himself from his reveries. The smile on her face told him the plot had thickened.

"What?"

"You know the post office by Peace Park?"

"Yes?"

"Well, there was a fight there between some Arabs who'd come to collect their social security checks and an American guy who lives nearby. He came to tell them it wasn't cool that they'd set the park on fire."

"He just went to the post office to tell them that?"

"Exactly."

"That's funny."

"Until we get the official report on the fire, want to check and see if the American was right?"

"I'll drive."

The brothers Sajad and Amar Abu Jalus didn't have Israeli passports. They did have an alibi for the time of the fire—they were on a renovation job in Givataim. Lozovsky left the assailants to the border police, then turned to the nearby ambulance, inside of which Jeremy Rodenstein was holding a cotton ball to his broken nose.

"Mr. . . . Rodenstein? I'd like to ask you a few questions."

Jeremy Rodenstein nodded.

"Hebrew or English?"

"Is that your first question? My Hebrew is excellent."

"Okay. Did you have reason to believe the two Arab men you spoke to at the post office were the ones who'd set fire to the park?"

"I didn't talk to them."

"Who did, then?"

"My son, Idan."

"And where's he?"

"He ran away after I defended him."

Lozovsky couldn't help but smile. He pictured Idan Rodenstein as a younger, more arrogant, yet more fearful version of his father.

The conversation was soon over. Cathy gathered a photo of Idan as well as his phone number. They got into the squad car and Cathy sighed. "Rodenstein's wife says Idan took her wallet and her car. Falafel?"

Lozovsky started the engine, drummed his fingers against the steering wheel, and confirmed, "Falafel." The French Hill falafel stands were a pilgrimage destination for northeastern Jerusalem's police force.

The nearest one had a long line of English-speaking students waiting outside, so they walked over to the next falafel stand. While Cathy placed their order, Lozovsky looked around, searching for any clues about the fire and the fight that had taken place just a few blocks away. Nobody seemed to care.

* * *

The next day was uneventful. Idan Rodenstein had yet to show up, and neither did any suspected arsonists. Lozovsky didn't want to leave the station, and certainly didn't want to go to French Hill. Something there had annoyed him, and he could only assume it was the residents. He knew how to handle Arabs, orthodox Jews, and right-wingers. But when faced with the bourgeoisie of French Hill, he felt like a caricature of a police officer. In their eyes, he recognized the combination of loathing for the police and an expectation of being nonetheless protected by them when need be. Like everyone else in Jerusalem, they knew a day would come when no one would run to their aid, and so community mattered. In French Hill, community meant culture, not accountability. Not blood.

The following day, Jeremy Rodenstein called and told them that his son was home and ready to answer questions. The investigation had reached a dead end, and Lozovsky was curious to know what kind of son would abandon his father to an angry mob.

He and Cathy drove over in the squad car, passing all of the falafel stands on Etzel Street, then Hagannah Street, Ghetto Fighters' Street, Bar Kokhva Street.

The sign on the door announced in English: *Welcome to the Rodenstein Residence.*

Lozovsky knocked on the door, waited, then rang the bell. A boy opened the door, looking like a hunched but intense version of his father.

"Idan Rodenstein?"

Idan Rodenstein looked at Lozovsky, then at Cathy. "Yes."

"We'd like to ask you a few questions about what happened earlier this week."

"I was at school on Monday, and then I went to see my geography tutor."

Lozovsky tuned in.

"We're talking about Tuesday," Cathy barked, "when you ran off and left your father to get beat up by the Arabs you provoked. Remember?"

The boy's eyes moved to Cathy again. "Yes, I remember."

"What was the deal? Do you know those people?"

"I saw them watching a video of the fire on a phone and laughing."

"A video of the fire?" Cathy repeated.

Lozovsky gave her a look as if to say that there was nothing there, and took the lead: "Do you speak Arabic?"

"Why would I speak Arabic?"

"I'm just checking. So you don't actually know what they were saying."

"I don't need to speak Arabic to know they were happy about it."

"So what did you tell them?"

"I said, *You like watching Jews burning*."

"And then you just left your father there?"

"I didn't just leave him there," the boy said, mimicking Lozovsky's tone. "We started walking away, but he was too slow."

That was enough for Lozovsky.

On the way back to the station, Cathy found the video of the fire on her phone. A neighbor had taken it from his balcony, adding the caption, *Terrorist arson in French Hill, June 17, 2003*. The video had been shared hundreds of times, along with different iterations of the sentiment, *Inshallah, let all of Jerusalem burn*. These captions appeared in Arabic, in Hebrew, in Arabic transcribed into English, along with literary passages and emojis. It was enough evidence to start an incitement investigation if they wanted to, but that wasn't the cops' major concern at the moment.

Cathy put down her phone and asked Lozovsky why he thought it would lead to nothing.

"That idiot Idan Rodenstein incriminated himself even before he said that."

Cathy was finally catching up.

Back at the station, they started cranking the wheels of bureaucracy to get hold of the security footage aimed at the wall. Lozovsky remembered quite clearly the conflict over the name, how people called it either a wall or a fence according to their political agenda, accusing the other side of twisting reality. And so now the two names had become interchangeable: a wall is built in Jerusalem, and this wall is called a fence on the Israeli side. It is also comprehensively documented through the use of state-of-the-art technology.

The day ended with a feeling of satisfaction. Lozovsky was always surprised when a case was cracked by a combination of police persistence and randomness. He just had to be stubborn enough to allow human chaos to leave gifts at the doorsteps of the just. That's how he saw things. That's how Stern and Felsner had caught the perps who'd thrown Molotov cocktails at university buildings. It was how Rajuan and Danon had caught the car hijackers in the area. And now it was Cathy's and his turn.

Lozovsky didn't think much about these things on Friday.

With great effort, he had set a line for himself between work and his private life, even if this line was more like a fence, or a wall, cutting him off from his family, his friends. He used the personal price he was willing to pay as the explanation for his professional success.

And so he spent most weekends in deep fog. But that Saturday morning he jolted awake, realizing an obvious truth. They would have dropped the violent incident at the post office if Jeremy Rodenstein hadn't alerted them to the return of his prodigal son. The alibi the boy gave them must have also been given to his father, who knew it was a lie but couldn't act on his own right.

Lozovsky got out of bed and went into the living room, where he sat down with his newspaper, his coffee, his sliced vegetables, and his bread and cheese, but he couldn't let go of the emotions he had about the case. There was no doubt in his mind about the findings that would soon turn up, but he didn't sense that any change to the power dynamic would follow. And if he didn't contribute anything to the good guys, what reason did he have to dedicate his life to them? All of his efforts and good intentions were but dust raised by the battling Jerusalem titans.

Cathy was startled when she picked up the phone. Barring a tragedy, Lozovsky had no reason to call her outside of working hours. She'd been on edge, as if she'd known a call such as this would come sooner or later. He apologized and reassured her that he only wanted to chat. She didn't seem completely convinced when he asked her opinion of the Rodensteins, but the words piled up, softening the tension.

"It's hard to raise children in Jerusalem," she said. "You have no idea what it takes."

"Maybe it's just hard to be a Jerusalemite," he countered.

"No, no. Being a Jerusalemite is the easiest thing in the world, but when you have a family, you start thinking that things need to improve."

The security footage arrived on Sunday morning. Lozovsky and Cathy checked one camera after the next, noting certain details, formulating a picture of the area before it had been consumed by the fire. They watched the empty park for minutes on end. No movement was registered save for a light breeze that shifted the swings, signaling the passage of time. Then, in a seventeen-second collection of pixels, Idan Rodenstein could be seen clearly, looking this way and that, pouring liquid out of a bottle, then lighting a flame.

Lozovsky smiled and cursed.

Cathy said she was sure he still had the lighter.

They kept watching the video footage. Different angles allowed them to put together Rodenstein's route from his home to Peace Park and back, his expression unchanging. They wondered if what they saw on his face was smugness or boredom.

Cathy called Jeremy Rodenstein and asked him to make sure both he and his son were home in the next hour. She shared their findings with him, and when he asked in a broken voice what was going to happen, she assured him that everything was going to be all right. Then she wondered out loud why she'd said that.

From that point on, they made sure to do everything according to protocol, cutting no corners. Lozovsky started the paperwork.

VAGINA

BY NANO SHABTAI

Jerusalem Forest

The *Sensual Woman* is open on the roof. First, she has to make whipped cream, with sugar and vanilla bean. Then she has to smear it carefully all along the penis and the testicles. She has to coat the entire area. Then, she has to lick it all clean. She has to start at the shaft. No, she has to start at the balls. Yes, yes, now she has to lick the cream off them. When they're perfectly clean she has to move up to the shaft, then slowly glide her tongue up in circles until she reaches the top, which she will suck intensely. At this point, the man should "climax." But the most important element of this exercise is to do it all with brief, gentle licks, like the fluttering of wings. That's what it's called: "The fluttering of the butterfly." If she is watching her weight, she should buy light cream. She could also top it with coconut, crushed nuts, or chocolate sprinkles.

Summer vacation will be over in a week, but we still have a big Scouts field trip ahead of us. The EDN gang—Elinor, Dana, and I—is waiting with bated breath. We have to take our revenge on Vagina. Elinor is the schemer and we're the executors. Why? Because nobody likes Vagina. Well, maybe the teachers do. Vagina is a total dork. She came here a year ago and lives in Efrat's house, because Efrat and her parents are on a government assignment in Canada. Before that,

Efrat was part of our group, and we were called EDEN. Poor Efrat, she doesn't even know if they're going to come back. "Depends on how well we fit in," is what her parents told her. They're so gross. During summer vacation, we wrote her a letter and took turns decorating it. I wanted to send her another letter, just from me, but I wasn't sure Elinor would like that.

Efrat's house is so pretty. It's on Reuben Street, right next door to Elinor's. I live on Shimon Street and Dana lives on Shimshon Street. Efrat's house has two floors and even a tiny attic, so sweet, where a real live servant used to live. My mom told me. There's super-soft grass and stone paths in the yard, and everything is surrounded by a tall wall, and even the plants that grow inside are so high that you can reach in from the street and pick a rose or just get scratched.

We were very angry when Vagina and her family took over Efrat's house like that. Efrat's room was so big. Before they went on their assignment we used to hang out there, playing *Monopoly*, drawing, making up quizzes, reading books. We'd stay for lunch or just fill up on sour green apples from the tree in the yard. At Efrat's birthday party her parents served Mozart chocolates. It's the best chocolate in the world. Now we meet on Elinor's mom's roof. It's the shed's roof, not the house's roof. We have a mat there and the damson tree protects us from the sun, as well as from Elinor's mom, though Elinor claims her mother doesn't truly care about anything— meaning, about what Elinor does and where she hangs out— even though she's a psychologist so she's supposed to care, or maybe it's exactly *because* she's a psychologist and has to listen to people cry all day—sometimes we see them walking out through the gate, looking all miserable—that she can't be bothered anymore. I don't know. The real question is, what are we going to do in winter, when the damson tree can't protect us anymore?

We shut *The Sensual Woman* and decide to go spy on Efrat's bedroom. Elinor's roof is right over it. The thing is, Vagina's father is a gynecologist. That's why we started calling her Vagina. It's so gross. Elinor gave her that name and explained what it meant. Now Efrat's bedroom is Vagina's father's clinic, and we can see all the women who go there. We see them walking through the green gate, and we see them sitting in that big black chair of his, their backs to us. We see him perfectly. We have binoculars and we're saving for a second pair so that we don't have to take turns so much. We can't let him see us, of course, but on the other hand there isn't really anything to worry about. We've spied on him enough times to tell he can't see a thing. Besides, he's like Vagina, with those glasses and that black curly hair. A gross dad.

The next day, we arrive at the Valley of the Cross at six in the morning. Dana's parents drop us off in the parking lot and we climb up to the camp, carrying our enormous backpacks and sleeping bags. The counselors stack wooden planks and take breaks to come back down to meet the buses that can only make it as far as the parking lot. Vagina has a bubble gum–pink sleeping bag, because Vagina is all about pink and purple. We've hated pink for a long time now. One can wear purple by itself, but definitely not pink. It's best to wear dark blue, dark green, black, and gray. Actually, it's fine to wear any color, including red. But not pink—never pink. In third grade there was a trend of pastel shirts—baby-pink, mint-green, banana-yellow, sky-blue, and lilac-purple. All the girls had those shirts with a bunch of different patterns: stripes, plaid, circles, all sorts of shapes. I didn't have one, because my mother objects to shopping. I don't want to get into that right now, but she accidentally washed an orange rug with one of my white T-shirts, dying it an unusual bright orange, and all the girls complimented it, never noticing I didn't have a pastel shirt like theirs. Not that any of that matters anymore. We'd never wear pink now, not even as pajamas.

We're going to camp in the Jerusalem Forest and come back in two days. We eat just a tiny bit of our candy on the way there because we want to save it for the way back. Gummy Bears, Bissli Grill, and Kefli snacks. Kefli is gross. I have a Pesek Zman chocolate bar in my bag and it got all smooshed but I still eat it and have to finish the whole thing at once because it is too crushed to save. Elinor says I look like I've been licking poop, but we have a great time. We scream every song so that our voices will be hoarse by the time we get home, and Elinor tosses some snacks at the front seat, where Vagina is sitting with our counselor, Daphna. Daphna stands up and shouts at us to cut it out, though not too seriously, because she doesn't want to spoil the fun. Elinor can be really insulting sometimes, but then a minute later she can be the most caring friend, so it's no big deal. She's also super smart and I don't get how she didn't pass the gifted-and-talented test. She really does know everything.

Then we get to the forest. I don't like hiking. I once went with my family to this mountain covered in purple lupine flowers and couldn't be bothered to climb it. I could see the flowers just fine from the bottom, so what was the point? Mom was so surprised, because I never used to complain— that's what she said. As we walked up the mountain she told me about her friend "from junior high" who once got her period on a school trip and spent the whole time with cotton wool fastened to her underwear with a safety pin. Why did I need to hear about that? It was gross, and generally speaking, "period" is the grossest word ever. Even grosser than "vagina." But hiking with the Scouts and my group is a different story, because Dana and Elinor are always so funny, and even though we have to keep our eyes on the ground to avoid tripping over a rock or walking into a thorn bush, it still goes by super fast, and by early afternoon we're already building the camp, which is the best part, helping the counselors with the beams and the knots. Elinor yells at me because I accidentally almost drop a beam on her foot, even though I don't actually end up doing it, and I say I'm going to get some water.

When I'm by the water and juice jugs, Daphna appears next to me and wipes my eyes. I have no idea what she wants. Then she says, "You're very sensitive, aren't you?"

I don't answer. Me? Sensitive? No way. I go back to my group and help build the biggest fire inscription we'll be burning that night, which spells out the words *Be prepared*.

That night, we talk about our changing bodies. At first Dana and I say changing bodies are gross and boobs are gross, because we don't have any, but then we realize we've made a big mistake, because Elinor is already starting to develop. I guess that makes her change her mind all of a sudden and she starts saying how a woman's boobs are beautiful, maybe the most beautiful thing in the world, that sort of stuff. We say, Sure, that's true, but not when they're too big. That's fine. She also says they are intended for feeding babies, which we never even thought about, and we're all obsessed with babies, crazy about babies, even though none of us have babies at home because our brothers and sisters are all grown up and annoying, but we still can't say that babies are gross because they're the tiniest and cutest and sweetest things in the world. But periods are still gross. Elinor says "period" and none of us want to get it. "Period" is actually an okay word. Before we read *The Sensual Woman* we read a book in English called *The Human Body*. It also belonged to Elinor's mom, and Elinor translated it for us, but we didn't learn much from it. Most of the time we just looked at those two awful pages covered with pictures of penises. There were a million types of penises: a short, fat, white one; a long and skinny one with red hair all around; and penises with a kind of point at the end; and one that ended with a round shape like a used-up pencil eraser; and all sorts of other shapes and colors. It was just the grossest thing imaginable. The grossest thing I've ever seen. Dana said she felt like throwing up, but she didn't. We looked at it every time we went to Elinor's house. We could really picture the person attached to every penis, whether he was fat or thin, pale or tan, and how ugly he was.

Something super weird happens on the second day of the trip. First thing in the morning, Elinor walks up to Vagina by the water jugs while we're brushing our teeth and washing our faces, and asks her if she wants to hang out with us today. We keep staring at her on the way to breakfast, all confused, but Elinor whispers, "I know what I'm doing." We trust her with our eyes closed, as people say. Completely.

Vagina actually does hang out with us, and we ask her a ton of questions as if we're really her friends. She tells us all about where she used to go to school, how she plays the mandolin and goes to Chess Club, how she wants to get a dog but her parents won't let her. She's so weird, Vagina. She's also gifted and talented, and goes to the G&T program once a week. My mom wouldn't let me take the entry test, she's against it, so I don't know if I'm gifted or not. Elinor was so mad when she didn't pass the test, though her mom told her it didn't mean anything and that each person is gifted in her own way.

We even pee together with Vagina, at a spot far away from the path that has these high weeds that poke and tickle our vulvas. Vagina crouches ahead of me and I look at her butt. It's so white, but it doesn't have any freckles, like her face does. She has these black freckles on her face. Gross. But not on her butt. I see her pee dripping down, and she squats until the drops stop, still as a statue. I'm not careful enough and get pricked by nettles. Dana always pees the fastest, we can't figure out how she does it. Elinor uses a big leaf to wipe herself and isn't embarrassed at all. She pulls her underwear back on standing up. There are all sorts of ways to go in nature.

That night, we light the fire inscriptions: *Be prepared* and the name of our tribe, *Beacon*. We eat burned potatoes and marshmallows, canned corn, and fish sticks we all end up tossing in the trash along with the plates after only one bite. I actually like the way they taste, but I toss mine in the trash too. We drink a ton of sugary juice the counselors make, apricot and raspberry. Elinor says that in the middle of the night we're going to get up and light a fire all our own, away from everybody else—she already found a private spot, a kind of clearing—and have a ritual for Vagina. It's going to be a surprise for her. I can't tell if she means a good surprise or a bad surprise.

In the middle of the night we wake up Vagina and tell her we're going to have a ritual to accept her into our group. Vagina doesn't want to get up, but we don't let her get away with that. We pick her up inside her bubble gum–pink sleeping bag until she finally sits up. Then we place a crown of pink and purple dead nettles on her wild black curls. The path leading to the top of the mountain has already been lit up with a string of sand lanterns, and we lead Vagina all the way up to the bonfire Elinor lit all on her own. She also lifted a bottle of wine and a pack of menthols from the counselors. We each take a swig of wine and share a single cigarette, coughing our lungs out and laughing like lunatics. Now we know for sure we'll be hoarse by the time we get home. We dance around Vagina, singing Scout songs, like, "*Corny, corny, corny, Sarussi is so horny! Corny, corny, corny, Sarussi is so horny!*" Sarussi is the boys' counselor and normally only the boys sing that song, but now we sing it and sing it until finally Elinor cries, "That's enough!"

Now it's time for the apple. We step away from Vagina and the bonfire. Elinor points out a good spot. We all duck down to take a shit. It takes awhile, but we get it done. Elinor clicks on the lighter and picks up the apple. We each take a bite in turn. Elinor takes the biggest one. Then she ducks down and dips the apple in poop. "Let's go!" she says, and we return to Vagina, who is sitting like a statue in front of the bonfire, saying nothing.

Dana offers her the shit-dipped apple. Vagina doesn't know it's covered in shit, but she still hesitates. Elinor tells her we already had some and now it's her turn. When Vagina finally takes a bite and chews it loudly, we don't say "Gross" or even raise an eyebrow. We just stand over her while she eats and eats and finally swallows it all down. When she's finished and still says nothing, we start singing again: "*For she's a jolly good fellow, which nobody can deny!*"

Then Vagina starts shivering. Her shoulders tremble. She

might be crying, but she makes no sound. We pause, and then Elinor starts singing again, so we join her: "*Happy birthday to you! Happy birthday to you! Happy birthday, dear Vagina! Happy birthday to you!*"

Back home, I go into my little sister's closet and grab my old pajamas, the ones I recently gifted her. I don't say good night to anyone because I've lost my voice. My sister is asleep, and the pajamas no longer fit me, so I roll them up and tuck them under my head, like a pillow. They're pink.

SEVEN WAYS TO MAKE JEWISH STUFFED FISH

BY YAARA SHEHORI

Mishkenot Sha'ananim

Three days after the festival ended, they started shooting at Jerusalem. And then they started shooting in Jerusalem. The days were very hot and the difference between *at* and *in* seemed merely semantic. A man with a white scarf ran, his face bloody. It wasn't actually a scarf, but a torn shirt that dangled around his neck and bare torso. And yet, as long as a festival was in session, Aya forgot this was a city where people could shoot each other in the street. Where something like that was even conceivable.

Six days after the festival ended, three babies died before dawn. Then the children died. But not that night, no, not yet. She knew those children were discussed later, in the business classes of the airplanes returning the writers to their home countries. But when the whole thing started, the babies were still breathing, and people were still hesitant to call it a war, and most of the participants had already extended their stay in Israel, making a vacation of it. The flights were long, the writers hadn't been to Israel in years and years, some not since childhood, when they'd come as part of some youth mission or family visit. There really was no point in trying to calculate the passage of time, even if some of them had visited year after year, summer after summer. Now they stayed a few days longer in a room with a balcony that overlooked not the walls of the Old City but rather—full disclosure—the Tel Aviv beach. Aya knew this. She handled their schedules as well as the slight booking confusion. Susan admitted it was a mess and blamed the Middle East.

Speaking of blame, Susan Meirson had warned her in advance that this was going to be a "serious headache," still using English phrases loosely translated into Hebrew, but Aya didn't believe her. They handled PR for the Jerusalem Literary Festival, as well as some of the outdoor events for the Israel Festival and the Jerusalem Film Festival, where Aya had found herself guiding an elderly European director who had gotten lost in the hallways of the Jerusalem Cinematheque. But Susan said writers were something else. Lots of problems. Lots of neuroses. Lots of talent too, obviously, she added in a tone Aya couldn't quite decipher. But insufferable. Except for Rushdie, she said. Rushdie was absolutely perfect. Aya couldn't tell if she was joking.

Susan Meirson ran a Jerusalem office. That was the branding, before branding was even a thing, in spite of the fact that Susan Meirson came from California with her long gray hair, which she claimed to wash with horse shampoo, along with her white button-downs that flapped in the back, ahead of her time in Israel, and therefore often appeared a bit unkempt. "It's no wonder," said those who bought into the myth that she was a distant relative of Golda Meir. "Golda didn't care about things like that either."

Publicly, Susan never bothered to dispel the rumors of a familial connection. Yet to Aya, who didn't dare ask, she confessed: "We Meirsons aren't related to anyone. Just simple Jews, no wars."

But Susan was a distant friend of Shira, Aya's sister, who advised her on legal matters. And it was because of this friendship, or perhaps because of the legal advice, that Susan hired Aya for a part-time position as her assistant. Aya's film studies had dissipated into the thin mountain air around the time that Shira went on maternity leave from her position as a public defender. She promised Aya things would work out fine. Susan would take care of her.

From the moment she set foot in it, she was baffled at how Susan Meirson's business could possibly survive. It was run from a tiny space on the edge of the Rehavia neighborhood. It was more like a place to receive letters than a place to run a business from. Not that anyone ever sent letters, though they certainly sent packages. There was almost nothing in the office of Susan Meirson Jerusalem Public Relations apart from a tiny sofa, two potted plants, and a signed movie poster from 2003. Most of all, the office was filled with Susan Meirson's red mouth. She knew how to look serious and facetious at once, making her clients feel included in a private conspiracy. Smoking was allowed. Children were not. Aya, referred to by her older sister as "the baby," was introduced this way to Susan, even though Shira already had a real baby of her own. In spite of this, Aya got the job.

She attended the semiformal prefestival dinner, which included some of the most successful, most Anglo-Saxon, and most strikingly Jewish writers that took part in the festival, three categories that, oddly enough, often overlapped. No one there had any children, not even the couple who had cowritten all of their books. They kept their division of labor a secret. (Did he write landscape descriptions while she wrote dialogues? her sister had once theorized mockingly.) Some people said that he was the talented one and she was the hanger-on, and others claimed that he was the one riding on her coattails. The more they succeeded, winning prestigious awards, the more brightly they shone, the more everybody agreed that neither of them had any real talent whatsoever. And the more they were disparaged, the more people awaited their arrival, the way one breathlessly awaits movie stars. She pictured them later, on the airplane, after everything had already been made public. They had tried to get an earlier flight but ended up spending two more days in sunny Tel Aviv, just as it had appeared on the Ministry of Tourism's website. He must have cried upon seeing the photograph of the dead babies, his fair hair fading. He looked like the type.

A week after that dinner, images of Israeli soldiers patrolling the city were seen all over the world, and the writer couple issued a statement that it was a tragedy. Jeremy Zimmer, the young Canadian author, tweeted a photograph of the soldiers along with the caption, *Not in my name.* Aya, who was still following him, recalled how she'd made little handwritten place settings with the names of the writers who attended the festival, including his. It was old-fashioned and charming, and like all things old-fashioned and charming, it had been Susan's idea. The executive producer who was sitting around, waiting for his meeting with Susan—who was running fashionably late—paused behind Aya as she was working on the place settings, his shadow falling on the cream-colored stock paper. Over her head, he said to Susan Meirson, who had just walked in, "If a terror attack happens there, it'll be the end of young Jewish American literature!" Susan didn't seem to hear him. "And Israeli literature!" he added. Susan offered him a smile that Aya was already familiar with and walked over to him very slowly. There were final arrangements to be made for the panel of three American writers, the ones the producer had already eulogized.

"I can't believe you work in PR now," Shira said after

Susan had hired Aya, as if she had nothing to do with it. "I thought PR people were supposed to be fast and smooth."

"We're the new generation of PR," Aya explained. "We aren't pretty or sweet."

"Oh." Shira peered at her sister. "Unfortunately for you, you *are* kind of sweet." She reached over and picked up the baby, who was writhing in her sister's arms, a pale and tender child who made her mother sharper and more agitated than ever.

The sky had started to darken and the tables in the heart of the market were covered with white cloths, reminding her of cars wrapped in covers to protect their bright paintwork from the scorching sun. The menus were printed by typewriter and the chef was dancing behind the bar, white apron around his waist, arms bare. Susan liked to bring her guests here, especially when the check was picked up by the Ministry of Diaspora Affairs or the Ministry of Culture, though the good old days of the 1990s, "when the budgets were great and we had no trouble getting real artists over here," were long gone. But Susan had adjusted. Aya hoped Susan wouldn't ask what she herself had been up to in the nineties. She hoped Susan would forget for a moment how old she was.

Most of the people around the table were wearing light-colored, well-cut clothes, like tourists on safari. The writer couple wore matching gray silk blazers with an effortlessness that Aya still didn't understand was the result of a life entirely unlike her own, as well as money. Aya wore a black dress she'd borrowed from Shira, which was slightly too small. She felt the seams rubbing against her armpits. She was beginning to sweat.

They sat me next to him, Shira, she kept telling her sister in her mind, forgetting that, had her sister actually been there, she would probably not have judged Aya favorably. *They sat me there*, she thought self-righteously into the empty space, and with each repetition the statement dripped between her fingers, moronic. *They sat me there.* What are you, a doll at a tea party? But she sat there because Susan had told her in Hebrew, "Sit, sit," before repeating herself in English, in which the foreign command sounded softer, more bearable. So at the beginning of the evening, when she took her seat at the table, she still thought she was lucky.

Aya had spent the empty hours before dinner, when there was no point in returning to her shared apartment on the other side of town, sitting on the tiny couch at the Susan Meirson Jerusalem Public Relations office—Shira's dress hanging over her like a shadow—and reading a collection of short stories by the writer that Jeremy Zimmer had named as his favorite in a recent interview. Father and son reunite after a long time apart. They go in and out of restaurants, the father causing a scene, embarrassing his son with his nasty drunken behavior. Aya felt relief when she realized she liked the story, when she realized it was a story about love. She'd had time to read several of the stories in the collection, one of which had been adapted into a movie she'd watched in film school.

She'd bought Jeremy Zimmer's book as soon as it came out in Hebrew. It took place in a third Jerusalem that existed in some in-between space between Jerusalem Above and Jerusalem Below. His Jerusalem was populated with a collection of maimed people—hairless, limbless, sightless. Hunchbacks addressed each other in a mixture of Yiddish and English, attempting to build a temple as they hunted down kosher animals that had found themselves in this bizarre third dimension. They were all named rebbe. Rebbe Nahman. Rebbe Kalman. Rebbe Gershon. Before the dinner, she'd flipped through the book, once again reading the praise on the back cover, before she realized it was a comedy. A dark comedy. But she had no gift for the grotesque. She could never figure out what was funny about it.

Now she looked at his wrists, which were delicate and hairy. The conversation easily veered to and from politics, sketching circles around all the hot topics that would, in a matter of days, catch fire. The most famous writer of the bunch remarked that, when all was said and done, it was a stroke of luck that Kafka had never visited Israel. The long-necked writer who published flash fiction said that the notebooks in which Kafka had practiced writing Hebrew were utterly charming. She'd perused them that morning at the National Library. Once again, the question was discussed—what should have been done with his estate and who exactly had gotten their hands on it. Aya listened and tried to figure out why she wasn't enjoying herself. It certainly seemed like she ought to be.

Aya was, without a doubt, the least important person at the table. Once again she asked herself why she'd been invited there, since, from the moment she took her seat, Susan did not seem to need her at all. Aya examined the menu, which included no prices. Susan said, "He's a nice guy, a young Canadian. You'll find things to talk about. His book did relatively well." Now Aya wondered if Susan had seated them together not only because she knew Aya had read his book, but because Jeremy Zimmer was the least-known writer invited that evening. Even the Israeli writer in attendance, who had just told a joke, was more famous.

Drinks were served, most of which were garnished with

rosemary needles and mint leaves. Jeremy Zimmer kept looking at his phone and Aya tried to catch his eyes, turning her head in his direction, but it would have been easier to start a conversation with her water glass. Sitting at the head of the table, Susan recommended dishes that didn't appear on the menu while sharing a quick anecdote about the mayor of Jerusalem. Jeremy Zimmer didn't laugh. Aya had her own anecdote, about his favorite writer, known as the Chekov of American suburbia. When she finally addressed Jeremy, she really did feel like a talking glass. Perhaps she should have discussed the real Chekov? Too late, she recalled Susan's instruction: *Just pay them compliments. They can't resist compliments.*

"I loved your book."

For the first time, he glanced at her with a hint of recognition. "Which one?"

Aya considered pulling her copy from her bag. "*The Third Jerusalem.*"

"Well, it's the only one that was translated into Hebrew."

She confirmed she'd read the translation. "That scene where they pull the wall apart with their hands," she said. When she'd read it, she thought it was a poorly constructed metaphor, but now that literary stone wall was all she could remember from the book, holding on for dear life, climbing up and slipping back down. Aya sipped from the glass in front of her.

"That's my glass," he said.

"Ha," she tried to laugh. But that wasn't funny, either.

Jeremy Zimmer cleared his throat and looked at her askance. "You know, everywhere I go in the world, they seat me next to a nice Jewish girl. One who's marriage-ready." He looked her over, and she knew he'd picked up on her pit stains. "You're probably eager to have kids. How old are you, anyway?"

Aya tried to pretend she was someplace else, even just on the other side of the table, where the conversation had moved onto the subject of a new movie, even though most of the diners preferred old films.

Jeremy continued, "I suppose you're not the only one who has something to do with this. She's responsible too." He turned his gaze toward Susan, who was laughing uproariously, her hands on the table. Through his eyes, Susan probably looked crass and heavy, grotesque, more Israeli than American. But Aya had no gift for the grotesque. She looked down at her plate, entirely white apart from a drop of wine. She smudged the drop with her finger, turning wine into schmutz.

The long-necked writer was now speaking to the author wearing sunglasses. The male half of the writer couple was conversing with the most famous author at the table, their chat interrupted every few minutes when someone came over to shake his hand. She tried to guess who among them had heard what Jeremy had said. Then she imagined an army of desperate girls, their eyes like pairs of doves in a folk painting, pouncing on Jeremy Zimmer, grabbing his delicate hands. They came to him in twos from every desolate town where Jews resided: girls, followed by their towns' matchmakers, local versions of Susan Meirson, all overflowing with fat and self-satisfaction. Who knew better than she the hearts of the love-thirsty, affection-starved girls who simply *had to* marry the Jewish scholar who'd come to town.

Rebe Kalman and Rebe Nahman were already watching over Jeremy's shoulder, staring fearfully at the young women and their governesses as if they were about to swallow them whole. Aya thought about the only woman in Jeremy Zimmer's book—she didn't eat a thing.

She wanted to tell him that his allegories were meager,

his similes heavy-handed, that she'd never even consider reading any of his other books, and that his version of Jerusalem was even less convincing than this restaurant. She knew Shira would have come up with a witty comeback, or at the very least scolded her, *Cut it out, you're not a child.* Aya thought of Shira's baby floating in black water, a dollop of cream just before being swallowed.

Dinner was served. Everyone agreed it was wonderful. Jeremy addressed the man sitting on his other side amiably. It turned out there were seven different ways of making Jewish stuffed fish. She bit into a wrap whose contents she did not know. She dipped a spoon into the polenta. She chewed something defined on the menu as an ancient Kurdish pastry. For one moment, clear and awful in its certainty, Aya knew he was right. She really did want a baby.

The string of lights hanging over the writers on the other side of the table trembled and flickered, and Aya tried to recall how the story about the father and son had ended. She could have just left, but discovered that, in spite of everything she'd eaten, she had not a drop of energy in her body. Susan's gaze hovered over her.

The following week, all of this would shrink and dwindle, a dot marked with a pencil. She would see a man torn to shreds on the street, feel the dirt gathering at the city gates and on the scalps of children with her own fingers. The following week, none of them would still be there. She would sit at a table set for ten, night after night, doing everything alone. Jerusalem will fall, just like it always did. There are always reasons for falling.

Aya continued to sip from the glass in front of her, filled to the brim. "I'm sorry," she said, "I thought it was my glass."

PART IV

RETURNINGS

WHEN SLUMBER FELL ON ME

BY Tafat Hacohen-Bick

Old City

She handed the mikvah attendant her robe and took the stairs down in the nude. The water was pleasant, in spite of some hairs and a dead fly that floated in it. She fell into it, then let out all of her air desperately and screamed into the water, I can't take it anymore, I can't take it anymore, then louder, What am I going to do, God help me, what am I going to do? She only came up for air when her lungs were empty, then whispered a blessing for the dip, prayed for what she always prayed for, for light at home, to get back to the right bed, for their love to be good. But this time the words tasted salty. Above her, she heard a voice declaring, Kosher. She dove in again, deeper, and screamed into the water, I don't want to dip while I'm still sinning, I don't want to. If only things could return to their place.

When she came out of the water after the three dips, she looked into the attendant's eyes and thought, She wouldn't have done what I did. It's written all over her forehead. How tidy her house is, how she always remembers to soak the kids' stained clothes in time, how she always says the right thing. The attendant was slender and her skin was smooth and dark. She wore a very high headscarf and extra-thick brown tights. She wanted to ask the attendant to hug her, to whisper some words of comfort, to bless her, to infect her with the orderly skies above her head, but the attendant seemed to be very busy that day, only giving the fingernail check half a glance. Look at me! she wanted to yell. I may have had hair clinging to my back before I got in the water, you barely even looked. How can you abandon me today when I'm in this state?! But all the attendant said was, Health, fruit of your loins soon, amen. Then the attendant went into another room.

She walked out, dripping water all over the hallway, dried herself, and changed her white underpants for black ones, then whispered again some prayers for domestic bliss as she buttoned her shirt and wrapped her wet hair in the hood of her jacket.

As she walked outside, she was instantly enveloped by darkness. It was very cold and the roots of her hair burned. When she passed the synagogue, a sob escaped her and she barked at the darkness, What could I have done? I couldn't have done anything about it, you know, there was light, and I couldn't manage anything else, what could I have done, there was all that expectation, and I remembered him from all the other incarnations and thought I'd be able to fix everything, but I was wrong.

She wanted to walk inside and whisper a few words, but the synagogue was dark and shut, and she kept going, telling herself, That's it, I'm going home now, I'll keep my head down and walk inside. I won't leave all of my limbs on the doorstep this time. Enough with this begging, I've been a beggar for too many years, and all this hunger. She whispered to herself, So what if things have been etched too deep for too many years, perhaps even from a different lifetime? I have a good love and I'll make it work. He isn't going to disappear into the fog. He isn't.

It was pitch-black outside, and raining heavily. On her long way home through the flooded streets, beneath the dripping, ancient pine trees, she was glad to be washed again. She told herself, I'll come home different. I'll be different when I come to him. He deserves to have me different. I'll fall into his arms and forget everything, and I'll curl up inside his strong arms, and he'll caress the pain of this day away, and all the wings wrapped around me will become one wing, there will be no difference, it doesn't really matter, I just mixed the two of them up, what could I have done, I'll repair it, I'll lick all the shards, I'll glue all the pieces together.

When she opened the door she found the home quiet, lit up, and squeaky clean. How does he always know what to do? How does he always get it right? This is exactly what I need right now, for things to be soft and pleasant, to be taken care of, how wonderful this is. She wanted to jump up on him, to have him set her down on the clean kitchen table, kissing her neck, holding her with his beautiful arms and his tickling stubble, but David was busy. Without even looking at her he said, I'm stepping out to throw out the trash and maybe for a quick walk. Then he went out, leaving her alone with her desire.

She walked into the children's room and saw the four of them sleeping quietly, everything in its place, even the dolls lined up on the shelf, not stacked up in piles, the way she always put them away. She kissed each of the children and went back to the couch, turned on her laptop, read a little, waiting. What felt like a very long time went by, but David didn't come back, and she grew sad. Let him come back. I want him. What's with him? Why's he running out on me like this? But he didn't come.

She wanted to call, but told herself, Give him a minute.

Fifteen minutes later, she did call, but got his voice mail. Then voice mail again. Then again.

She sent him WhatsApp messages that went unread. What's with him? Why'd he shut everything down like this? What happened? She recalled what people said about the kind of people who held everything inside until they broke and everything fell apart all at once. God help him, something's wrong, something happened and he doesn't want to share it with me. How can I convince him to be with me if he doesn't pick up? She wanted to run outside and yell, David, David, where are you, David, I'm with you, David, but the kids were asleep and she couldn't go outside. What should I do? How can I find you, David?

She looked around and thought, If everything is this organized, that must mean he's planned a long journey. Where did you go? And why did you think it would be easier on me if you cleaned up everything first? She shouted into the darkness, What are you so mad at me for? What did I do? I whispered, I wrote a poem, I dreamed a lot, I skipped down the path, and I loved. Why are you so furious, and why won't you tell me? How could you just leave like that?

No, she thought. It's my fault. I played with fire and put us all in danger. I pulled you behind me on the tightrope, thinking you were going to be an acrobat like me, making it all the way to the end and even having a good laugh about it. I forgot how you always believe me. You saw a rope and thought, We're going to fall. You forgot how I always reach the end, how I laugh. It's my fault for putting us in danger, but who am I supposed to cry to now, to say, I'm sorry, there was a rope and I wanted to cross it, wanted to feel my heart beating and the sky close by, wanted to feel the fear of falling, and now I'm so sorry, I'll pack up the tightrope in a suitcase and only walk on wide sidewalks, keeping away from the road, just come home, I'm sorry. She wanted to tell him, You know that when I walk on tightropes I always fall into your arms, and that's my favorite thing, I like how you keep me safe, but you didn't understand that. I was so sure you knew all of it, and I'm sorry. Why are you disappearing on me exactly when I'm ready to come back? We're moving in opposite directions. The more I run to you, the more I lose myself in the fog, blind. Where are you? Where are you? She yelled into the darkness, but her voice was hollow and no answer came. Always with these different directions, as if we can't synchronize our watches. Once, I dreamed I was walking toward you with the wedding veil on my face. You handed me the wineglass. The sky was our chuppah. We shook hands in every world with no separation, and you were so glad, it was everything you wanted. I woke up happy and reached out to you, but you were sad because you had the opposite dream, and I could see in your eyes how I had run out on you all night long. I wanted to tell you, Of course I didn't! I was just coming to you! Why are we going in two different directions? But instead we got up, had coffee, made sandwiches, and hurried to drop the kids off at school, and you gave me a quick kiss so as not to hurt my feelings. What were you supposed to say? I'm mad at you because of my dream? What could you have said? But you *were* mad.

Where did he go now? Where could he go? I need to chase him. I need to tell somebody. But her arms were heavy, and all she did was think, Who could I possibly tell? And what would I even say? She wondered how she could call to him from a distance in her loudest voice, shaking up the universe with just the right tune, but the words shattered between her fingers, and the autocorrect kept changing things on her. She wanted to whistle through underground frequencies that would reach him and caress him just right, but nothing came out, and she dropped her hands and let go of everything, diving into bed.

Lately, a thought had been pestering her: that if they slept together constantly they'd be spared their sentence. They had sex in every corner of the house, as if signing an escrow on every square foot, confirming their lease was hermetic, on the couch, in the kitchen, in the shower, in the corner of the room, in the other corner of the room, on the floor, on the rug, in the cold, in the heat, sweating or shivering, standing up, lying down, fighting for their lives. She recalled the time she poured wine on him and then licked him clean, every corner of his body, as if, by painting herself onto every bit of him they'd last forever. She remembered how in the end they were very sticky and tired, and she thought, When love is so forced, one can't take it anymore. He was exhausted and left. He didn't say, Hang on, I'm tired, let's take a breath, let's let go of this struggle and just let love be sleepy and mediocre for once, without constantly resuscitating it, let's give it time to recalibrate. He didn't say that. Instead, he left. And now she couldn't fight anymore, everything was falling through her fingers, the glass was broken, and there was nobody to cry, This is a break from which one is born! Mazel tov and good health! It was all broken and wounded, and there was nobody to talk to.

I know I was wrong, she admitted. I thought I could taste every fruit without giving into temptation. To feel without falling too deep. I'd just forgotten a few rules for a moment there. Sometimes you realize too late that life has become dangerous, that you're at the center of a frozen lake, not knowing how you got there, or how to get back, and every move could break the ice, and you think, Maybe if I lie down and start crawling away no one will notice and I'll be able to escape slowly, silently, before the lake comes to life and buries me whole.

She spread her limbs on the bed, lying diagonally. Her body was empty and hollow, and she felt around: arm, leg, everything there, everything in its place. And yet she was weightless, as if nothing bound her to the bed. She rolled from side to side and thought, I'm so alone now in this empty night. It's going to be so long, in this horrible silence. She sank into the bed until finally she extricated herself, crawling into the children's room, curling up in bed with Miriam, holding her, trying to draw warmth from her. And she thought, I'll sleep, and I'll think about everything tomorrow morning. Tomorrow is going to be a new day. I'll take care of everything tomorrow.

The next day, when she saw that the car was gone too, she told the kids that Dad had gone to work early that morning, and that they'd have to hurry up and get to school by foot. They seemed to have read the stars in their sleep. They were tender, loving, attentive. She wanted to yell at them, Shout at me! Be mad at me! Things have broken in every world and it's my fault! But they were kind, helping each other along, dropping off at their respective schools too easily, offering sweet goodbye kisses.

Too early and too fast she was free and started walking, trying to weigh the possibilities: he'd gone to the desert, he'd gone up north, he'd gone abroad. She cursed herself: Why didn't I check if his passport is still at home? That should have been my first step. His phone was still turned off. She walked quickly, crossing Sha'arei Hesed, advancing toward downtown, toward Jaffa Gate, toward the Old City. All along she whispered to herself, I've got to call someone, his parents,

my sister, I've got to report him missing. But the street was
chilly and she wrapped her coat around her body and told
herself, Soon, soon, there's the Tower of David, after that
comes the Western Wall. I'll ask and I'll pray and everything
will be all right again. She started walking toward the Old
City Market but became swallowed in the flow of tourists,
following them down the alleyways, until she found herself in
the Church of the Holy Sepulchre. Enveloped in the calm-
ness of worshippers, she thought: This is all I wanted, to in-
dulge a little and then come back, it's just that I mixed up
the kingdoms, I'll fix it. She stood in line, hearing herself
crying among the mélange of foreign languages: God, help
me, make him come home, help me correct my ways, tell me
nothing is irreversible.

All of a sudden, she understood. Facing the corpse that
appeared in her mind, she knew she would never be able to
forgive him for this fear that now took hold of her. That was
unforgivable. Then she thought, How we've spoiled it. How
bad we've been. This was all one big mistake: We loved much
too much, but we always realized the pain too late. If only I
could love less and give up just once, making things just a
little less pretty and a little less painful.

She felt the cold blowing from the stones and tried to figure out what had taken place in the loneliness of last summer,
when the nights were hot and cold all at once. What could I
have done? I felt as if a river was flowing under the house, and
the street was filled with quicksand, and I was so alone, and
within that I wanted him just to be near me, do you understand? It wasn't instead of you, it's just that I wanted the way
he breathed on me, the way he leaned over me, whispering in
my ear, that's all, hearing him speak to me with this heat and
that, this rhythm and that. Do you understand? You know

that loneliness that trickles inside in midday and lodges in the throat, and if anything can alleviate it even just a little bit, how could I resist it? Just sitting together on a bench for a moment and knowing there's somebody else there.

She wanted to get out of there, to go home, to call David again, to find him and bring him home, to yell at him for all this fear he'd brought her, to shake him, to rage at him, but also to try to repair, to ask him if they could fix it. But the side room with the beam of light and the white curtain beckoned her and she went there like a blind woman following light, feeling with her hands, there's some light, I'm going to catch it. She was almost there, though she saw the step too late, and she tripped and fell, flattening out on the cold stone, and felt the blow to her forehead and brow. When she touched her hand to her face she realized, I'm bleeding, oh heavens, I'm bleeding too fast, I just fell, why does my blood have to make an appearance right away?

One of the tour guides ran over. Are you here alone? Do you need help?

She looked at him and said, I'm alone. To herself she said, We are always alone when our home falls apart, and we have no money and no job and no home, and we are naked, and we are alone.

Hang on, the guide said, I'll take care of you. He helped her up and sat her on a bench across from the beam of light, and gave her some water.

She drank and sighed. Why didn't I give up, even when I knew all our hearts were bleeding? Why didn't I get into bed with a little less feeling, just for once? Why didn't I realize that if blood flowed so much here, this might be too dangerous a place? Why didn't I take good enough care of you even when I did know? And why don't you take care of me now?

She took a deep breath and thought, I need to go to urgent care. I need them to look at my eyebrow. I need somebody to take care of me before this day is over. Before the kids come home. I need to bring David back, and I need to do the dishes, and I need to fold the laundry. I'm going to have to pick them up soon and put everything away. To the guide, who was watching her with concern, she said, I'll be all right, and I'll remember the way in spite of the mud outside. I'll get back home.

Slowly, holding the bandage he gave her against her eyebrow, she moved toward the exit.

When she reached Jaffa Gate she called her father. She wanted to say, Come over, Father, I need help today, come be with me, I'm all alone. But instead she whispered, I've never been smart, but I always wanted to be. What does that mean, Father? Why do I want so much? What should I do? I'm lost. I keep looking for new wisdoms and I'm never satisfied, I'm so hungry, Father, I've been hungry for so many years, what about wisdom? The library is so large and I'm tired. There's so much work to do. How much can one person learn? I've gone too far. I'm afraid I went the wrong way this time, Father. What should I do? I looked at the wrong books. How do I get back? I met a man with a very foreign, too-close wisdom, and I was enchanted. It had strange letters and unknown languages, and the words sounded so wise. I'm confused. I was wrong when I thought everything could be converted. I forgot to be careful even when the signs of idolatry were written on the wall, and even though you've always told me. But as much as you've warned me, I forgot how foreign he was and how not-mine, because he was also so familiar, and almost mine, I promise, it was so confusing, and I forgot all the prohibitions, what I was permitted, you see? What do I do now?

She sobbed, All I wanted was for him to hold me in his

arms and put me to sleep, to gather and soothe me, comfort everything that ached. I wanted to rest my head on his shoulder and hear him say, I'll take care of you now and I'll make everything all right, you can let go of everything, I'm here. That's what I wanted. I didn't mean anything else. I didn't mean for the hand to touch, for the tongue to lick, for the teeth to bite, I didn't mean for his intense look, the way he grabbed me, I didn't mean for him to pin me against the wall. I just thought: There's pain and there's love, and what could be so bad about that? For a moment I was bold enough to think I was also allowed to take comfort in this life. I didn't know that if I closed my eyes, all of this would happen. I didn't know that when I came close enough, he would suddenly take. I thought he'd never take, do you see? Privately, I called him Joseph. He was so righteous. But the body came nearer, and all this happened before I even noticed, and I didn't wake up before it was too late, and I heard his moan, and his body loosened, and I thought, There, I did the forbidden thing, I've offended the highest realms and now the world will fall apart. I limped home, my face grieving, and I washed my body, and thought about how sometimes one could just sleep in the middle of the world, and when slumber fell on me and intimacy was so sweet, I became intoxicated with the spicy honey and wanted to lick and bite, and I forgot all the prohibitions, because the fingers were warm and full of desire, and the body hardened and tensed, and it was so hard to say no, and I wanted to fall into a soft bed and let him caress me forever, but I didn't know the fingers would go so far, and that was a mistake. How could I have forgotten again everything I used to know?

I didn't catch any of that, her father said, the reception here is bad. He laughed. I'm glad everybody's doing okay. I'll talk to you later.

That really is the most important thing, she answered. Everybody is doing okay, and they are sweet.

How are you? he suddenly added. Are you all right? I get the feeling you need some strength today. Do a good deed, it helps.

You're right, I'll do a good deed today.

Charity. You can always donate to charity. That helps.

Charity. I'll donate to charity today.

Good, he said. So everything is fine.

Yes, good, she said. Everything is fine.

But just as she was about to hang up, he said, I found a painting you made one day when it was very cloudy and Jerusalem almost drowned. Remember? You were looking for the right colors and insisted on going off to look for that very dull white? Even though it was pouring outside, you wandered through all the shops, remember? It was such a beautiful painting and I hung it up over my desk, on that shelf you always say is going to end up falling on my head. Remember that painting?

WHY DID YOU CROSS THE LINE?

BY NADAV LAPID

Talpiot

The mad commander Lieutenant Colonel A, who, in his own dreams and mine, led thousands to take down tens of thousands and die themselves on the way, friends me on Facebook. When I approve his request, he likes my most recent post.

This happens many years, more than half a lifetime, after the last time I've seen him. Over time, he'd become the protagonist of a story I revised and expanded and which won me—thanks partially to Lieutenant Colonel A—some glory in limited circles, a fairly fine number of women, and some choice seafood platters, as I cursed and cursed him and his memory, until I'd forgotten he'd ever truly existed; that he always made sure to sit by himself in the outpost's dining hall when he ate his sunny-side-up eggs, so that it didn't run down his chin in front of his soldiers; that he had broad shoulders and a high-pitched voice; that he'd grown up in Haifa; that he was handsome; that he listened to operas (and not only the famous ones); that he prayed for war, not metaphorically speaking but truly prayed with devotion, standing on a sand dune overlooking the Damascus suburbs, swaying back and forth and murmuring, "Come now, Syrians, come."

Who would have believed that crazy commander was truly alive? And not only alive, but that he woke up in the morning, turned on his computer, logged onto Facebook, and decided who to friend.

I don't want to miss this moment, worried about the unsteady Wi-Fi connection on the train. Me: *Great seeing you after 26 years. How are you?* (a smiley face)

He doesn't respond. A month later, he sends a thumbs-up.

A month later, I think now. When I will lie in bed in the middle of the day, touching myself bellow the belly, I ponder here now, on the train, on my way to Grandpa's dad's shiva.

Grandpa's dad fell down and died.

Grandpa is known as Grandpa for the same reason any eighteen-year-old would be known as Grandpa. He started losing his hair in high school and developed all sorts of odd mannerisms more suitable for old people. It was hard to tell if he lost his hair first and then adopted the mannerisms or if he started with the mannerisms and the hair followed their lead, and if he'd exaggerated them because we encouraged him. But because, after he was honorably discharged from the military, Amit (Grandpa), like many of the outpost's soldiers, became a junior engineer for the arms industry—working for an electronic or ballistic warfare manufacturer—nobody bothered about him, so nobody knew.

His father, who made a point of distinguishing himself from the rest of our fathers and mothers, who were dropping like flies those days—from the new pandemic? From the old pandemic? Dad, Mom, and my aunt and uncle had been standing in the line of fire for several years now, while life treated them like its shooting range. But Grandpa's father went out to hang the laundry on a stormy night, as Edelman with the ears about whom I didn't really care (only Israelis think there are storms in Israel) wrote on the WhatsApp group, and slipped off the balcony, or the roof—the message wasn't clear.

I used to crawl my way to Jerusalem on a bus that rolled and rolled, there was nothing but the way. Jerusalem is an Ithaca without an island or a beloved, a journey without a destination. These days I race over on a train that, according to the Israel Railways website, leaves at 11:06 from platform 2. The doors closed at 11:06 and no amount of banging on the plastic helped. In this sense, humanity is chugging ahead while the latecomer stays behind.

Forty minutes to kill at the station.

Lots of soldiers eating cinnamon-raisin pastries that come free with a Coke Zero in a special deal. Including the soldier whose name the female-soldier-with-the-coffee-with-foam on his left didn't know but has just learned: Maor. They were in the same sector, in the same brigade. Her cousin, his cousin, a bite from the cinnamon pastry, that naughty girl took a bite right where all the raisins were clustered—this'll end very well.

One might add that these are the days of yet another military operation, when the entire country, and certainly Jerusalem, the queen of smut, is filled with *Death to all Terrorists, Jewish Blood Will Not be Spilled*, women in leggings and low-cut shirts who hate Arabs and love Lana Del Rey, nostalgic and sentimental music that fascists love, that idiots love, that I love.

I'm sitting on the train now. Next to me is an Ethiopian soldier with big sunglasses and a fighter's rifle, magazine attached with a black rubber band. Ever since I left for Paris I pronounced Israel dead to me and vowed never to look at it again, or if I did, then only through innocent or tourist eyes. Here I am now, practicing it, looking at the soldier and thinking, *Wow, women do military service too? They shoot rifles? At people? Have you ever killed a person? If that's how you shoot, I wonder what you're like in bed. Any chance you'll wear your uniform on our date? By the way, are you Jewish, if you don't mind me asking? I didn't know there were Black Jews. Interesting, three exclamation points. So what are you more, Jewish or Black? Don't answer that. How did you feel during Black Lives Matter?*

Once upon a time buses exploded in this city and many people paid for their desire to live an average life, just like everybody else. We went out to a bar downtown. We were two guys and three girls; the girls were all in love with each other through some invisible mathematics. It might have been winter, but for the sake of the story, say it was summer. Born Jerusalemites climbed onto the bar tables, kicking and stomping to the beat of "Jerusalem Praises," the techno version. There was still techno back then. One of the three girls dropped her head on the table, smearing her cheek all over it, and cried all night as sneakers rubbed up against her nose and her ponytail, stepping on her tears. The walls were big windows that would fly right into your jugular when the place blew up. We waited for the suicide bomber. Hours spent with our eyes glued to the front door. Let him come. Then he came. An Angel of Death paused at the door, wearing a long overcoat in the middle of summer (to hide his explosives, etc.), and we knew it was all over. He ended up asking for a beer. He was the bartender's fuck buddy.

Now none of that exists anymore. Lone bombers and exploding buses live on only in the online comments nutjobs leave at the end of *Ynet* articles and in TV series that need a surprising cliff-hanger.

On the WhatsApp group "Sorry for your loss, Grandpa," everybody texts: *On my way.* Vardi is not included in the

WhatApp group, which is precisely why he's about to emerge.

There was a line. They told him, "Vardi, go get the bottle."

"Which bottle?"

"The orange soda, you monkey!" Yaron D. shouted, and Amit Guerman mumbled, "Go left-right-left-right, hurry, Vardi, run over here and come back breathless, if you're not breathless you didn't run, but don't cross the line, roll it to us, roll it gently! It's fizzy, Vardi, if it sprays when we open it, you're a dead man."

Then they said, "Go get the strawberry passion-fruit, the bottle with the multicolored cap, just above where the last one was or just below, and come back faster this time, we're thirsty, what don't you understand?"

("Look at him, Guerman, even uglier than you.")

("Your mama's ugly, Yaron, I just saw her out to pasture with the rest of the cows.")

("Guerman, you birth defect, you mumbler, say it, don't spray it.")

"But don't get too close to the line, Vardi, roll it to us. Good. Now go get garlic toast"—made with the IDF-issued garlic powder that comes in eleven-pound sacks; that's how we were going to fuck up the Syrians, with garlic breath—"and use the fresh bread from the bag by the tunnel in the bunker. Cook it in the sandwich press with the fat cable. Not the one we used to grill that mouse—gross. Use the old one, the one that pops the fuse. Put it on a paper plate behind the line and blow on it. Blow on it until it crosses the line and reaches us."

They'd drawn the line with an anti-ecological deodorant spray bottle. The line divided a windowless twenty-six-foot room with bright-green neon-lit walls at the outpost. An impassable line of air, a line of scent, a scent which resembled, as I liked to imagine and so did everyone else, because we shared an imagination, as I masturbated all day long as we all did in the half-private showers about fat girls or skinny girls so we could make sure everyone else masturbated just like we did, the scent resembled . . .

"Permission to cross the line," Vardi said.

"What for?"

"To bring you the garlic toast."

"Push the garlic toast."

"Permission to cross the line."

"What for?" (I'd dozed off on the train and woken up. I'd dreamed something, roused from a heavy slumber, even though I'd slept for less than a minute.)

"To get some air," Vardi said, which was ridiculous because the room was sealed, and there was no air here or there or in the line, only a dense smell of everything bodies make. Guerman laughed his ass off with his spitting tongue. But Vardi insisted: "I'm crossing the line."

Yaron, whose wide face was going gray with boredom, stretched because sweet music started running through his ears, the kind of music that makes you feel that everything is just starting and that everything is still possible. "You're not crossing."

"I'm crossing."

"Go on," they told him. Or maybe: "Go on, you son of a bitch, we dare you to cross the line" (which was as imaginary and as robust as an electric fence). Guerman, whose brother got hit in the head by a boulder six months earlier, in Nablus, I think, and Yaron, who was inexplicably obsessed with 1950s American movies, Hollywood film noir. All of his crassness disappeared when he spoke about them, the insult on his thick face whenever anyone didn't know or didn't care about *The Maltese Falcon*. Later he'll become a cop, but not yet.

"I'm crossing," Vardi said, advancing about four inches toward the line, though to begin with he'd only been a foot and a half away from it on one side, while Guerman and Yaron were a foot and a half away from it on the other side, because we were all crowded, twelve people in a small room. "I'm crossing right now."

"Don't cross!"

"I'm crossing!"

"Don't cross!"

"I am!" Vardi screamed. Vardi, who was normally such a doormat, prescribing to that trite idea that weakness is in fact strength, and why did you insist so much? (Menachem Begin station, dozens of escalators spit you out into a construction site. Jerusalem blankets you with dust.)

Somebody, who knows who, said that in that moment there was another pair of eyes behind Vardi's, and that it was these eyes, the ones behind, that refused to back down, that forced him to advance, against his nature, another half an inch and another, until the nonexistent line that had been kissing the tip of his shoe now trailed four inches behind his heel. (I was surprised by that statement about the second pair of eyes. We didn't normally talk like that. We just didn't. We didn't know. We knew *cold hot hungry give me take it bed*. We were young and we were winners. We've all become orphans since.)

It's impossible to judge what happened next.

It's impossible to understand it without knowing that when Yaron couldn't fall asleep he'd spend his nights coming up with mean names for every soldier in the crew, based on their physical flaws, polishing the names, honing them, testing them on himself to see if they made him laugh and if they were sufficiently insulting, then waiting breathlessly till morning so he could use them, tossing and turning with excitement, lying awake for hours, giggling to himself. ("Elad, move your head, your nose is blocking Syria." A laughing fit. "Shai's ears are here, so he'll be arriving shortly.") You can't understand it without knowing that when new recruits showed up at the outpost he'd pray for there to be one with big ears, or too much bodily hair, one who sweats excessively, a short one, not to mention bigger flaws like crossed eyes, a facial birthmark, a tiny penis, etc. You can't understand without knowing that Yaron himself had a collection of physical flaws that made reacting to him obvious and available even to the shiest, most stuttering of soldiers. You can't understand it without knowing that this only egged him on. You can't understand it without knowing that, the spring we arrived on base, he called Vardi "the Black Goat," and then "an abducted Yemenite monkey." You can't understand it without knowing about the Yemenite Children Affair. You can't understand it without knowing that Vardi, mostly in retrospect, attributed clear ethnic motives to this conflict. You can't understand it without knowing that Yaron and Guerman both came from lower-middle-class Ashkenazi families, one from a commuter town up north, the other from a commuter town in central Israel, and that later in their lives they would become a beat cop and an economics teacher, respectively. You can't understand it without knowing that Vardi was the son of a famous commercial arbitrator up north, who had fair hair and looked nothing like his son (hence the "*abducted* Yemenite monkey"), and that Vardi would later make use of his connections in a real estate deal involving the command major general in order to complete his revenge. You can't understand it without knowing that even back then I watched all of this from a distance and from up high, untouched by either side. You can't understand it without knowing I was a prince (later diagnosed by two different psychologists as suffering from Prince Complex), which is why this all took place beneath me, involving me only by way of elimination.

Later on, after he received the typical punishment for crossing the line, or perhaps a little more than the typical punishment, Vardi's terrible rage bubbled up. As I mentioned, his father knew the command major general. The husband of his aunt was the corps commander's childhood friend. Yaron and Guerman were sent to carry bombshells as if they were sacks of flour. Not even shells, but unexploded shells, until they grew bent and hunched. "I want them walking with a cane by the time they turn thirty."

I hadn't heard from Yaron or Guerman ever since. People like to say that in this age of social media, people no longer disappear. Every old-timey literary mystery can be solved by a click of the keyboard. But I never heard from them again, and all I knew of them were remote rumors that had reached me during reserve duty service, where I lamented the three years of my youth that I'd spent in *I'm crossing the line don't cross the line I'm crossing the line don't cross it I am too don't,* all that muck. You walk into a half-closed public shower to bathe and masturbate, you come out, and your towel is covered with tiny cling-bugs that only exist in the military.

The rumor was that among the unexploded bombshells, Yaron met a beat cop, God knows what he must have done to deserve that punishment, and fell in love with the man's wife (it's so unlike Yaron to fall in love). In order to run into her at police events, he became a beat cop himself. He was on television once, the day Ariel Sharon went up the Temple Mount. Yaron was shown a moment before storming the Arab protesters, one of those panicked, violent faces. Who would have guessed we'd once dreamed of *Sunset Boulevard*?

And Guerman, who was always thinking about the magic of missiles in flight and would mumble indecipherably about them with his lisp, hurt his hips carrying those bombshells. (Cartilage? Slipped disc? He was weaker than Yaron but almost ridiculously committed to the task. I could picture him limping along with the shell in his arms, only collapsing after he'd reached his destination.) He became a teacher, and I can only imagine how badly his students make fun of him, mimicking his speech patterns.

We'll sit shiva together, I thought on the taxi or on the bus or on foot in Talpiot, thick buildings, gray in the sun, brown in the moonlight, where the deceased lives. I did not pause under the building to look up at the roof and try to catch a glimpse of the water heater that had betrayed him, nor did I picture his body's ballistic trail as it shot down to the sidewalk.

I climbed the stairs.

Some might cry, even Grandpa, yet it's strange to cry like that at his age, though he'd aged so much that the nickname no longer suited him. Every creaking of the front door would make us jump. *Is it them? Is it him? Come to settle the old score once and for all, like in a Western?* As if we truly wanted to know if everything that had happened to us had truly happened.

I'd spend all night waiting to see if the two showed up, if the one showed up, if that line drawn through the air, drawn with scent, would rise again, as if redrawing the line would bring the mother back to life so she could put on a mask and blab about COVID like everyone else.

Why did you cross the line back then? And why did *you*, Mom?

Grandpa's dad, who for some reason insisted, at age eighty-one, to hang a shirt to dry on the boiler on the roof and fell down, would still be alive, and the mother would know his son and his father would not be lonely.

They once went to visit him in Paris, the mother and father. Her disease was running rampant but nobody knew. They came to Paris and I was very busy, though I managed to get them a place with a glass ceiling, a cute apartment I was proud of; the only downside was that it had a spiral staircase. I told Mom, "Watch yourself on those stairs," and she held onto the railing and took very good care not to fall, slowly raising and lowering her body, which was already being burned on the inside by a great big lump of death.

It was a difficult day. Late that night, already in bed, toward the end, he'd receive a text message from her: *Oh, Nadav, the rain is so beautiful. I'm sitting in the living room and watching how the drops of rain fall down the roof.*

LEVY

BY Tehila Hakimi

National Library

> *. . . Johnny said that if it were up to him, Jacob wouldn't see the light of day. "You wouldn't see the light of day." Then he popped him with one awful blow and left him there, in a puddle of blood. No one would be coming to the stacks before Sunday, he thought. And no one would be looking for Jacob over the weekend. He knew Jacob had no special plans. The guy had told him he wasn't going to spend Shabbat with his parents. Then Johnny slammed the warehouse door, locking it behind him. He hurried toward the elevator . . .*

She didn't notice him right away. She was so focused on the attempt to write one more word, one more sentence, that she didn't look up from the screen with its near-empty Word doc, glowing cruelly. At least she'd managed to put together these first few lines, she thought. It seemed that her greatest fear was about to come true: now that she'd finally found the time for it, her writing was stalling. She was blocked.

As the weeks went by, her fears grew worse. She was afraid of becoming like one of those writers she abhorred—the tortured ones, the ones burdened by writing, the ones who complained about it in every interview or panel discussion.

Levy always sat in the same spot—the last table in the

row nearest the staircase. Bent over a book or a notepad, a stack of books in front of him. With each passing week, his stack grew higher, hiding more of his already wiry body. He placed the books so that people passing by his table couldn't make out their titles.

She didn't know his full name. Not then. Not until she found out through that newspaper item: *The police are requesting the public's assistance in their search for Levy Yitzhak Greenspan, last seen at Hillside Supermarket wearing a black suit, brown shoes, and a black hat.* In the accompanying photo, his gaze was so smoldering that for a moment she didn't recognize him. Black eyes, dark hair, average height, the piece stated. But the man who sat in the reading room every Tuesday had gray-green eyes, a soft gaze, and an ever-shortening beard.

The truth was, from the moment she saw him, she could not ignore his presence, even though they'd never exchanged a single word. Most of the people who used the library reading room avoided eye contact. But she knew she'd have a use for him anyway, for his character, who had appealed to her from first sight.

That day, she was so glad to finally return to her writing. At the top of the page, she wrote those cutting words, the ones that hadn't let go of her since the first time she'd read them. This time, she felt she'd finally fulfilled the potential they'd planted within her. She didn't mean to just leave them there. *I shot him between the eyes.* That line that appeared twice. *I shot him between the eyes.* She knew that, just like Ginsburg, her story had to start at the end, then make its way back to the beginning.

When Levy got up and headed out of the reading room, she followed him, first with her eyes, then she jumped up and walked out after him, leaving her belongings scattered over the desk. She didn't even shut her laptop. She was only a minute behind him, but couldn't find him near the library's main entrance, her eyes searching in vain. She only saw him after she took the stairs down toward the bus stop. He was waiting there. Who's he waiting for? she wondered. She sat down on the steps. And who are those two people in the stacks, she hadn't decided yet, and why did one punch the other like that? The image was clear but the motive was not. That's all right, it's only the beginning, she told herself. It'll come to you soon, it always does, you just have to keep going. She thought what a pity it was she'd quit smoking. It was boring on those steps. She'd even left her phone on her reading room desk.

Some time later, a bus pulled up at the station and several boys and girls, probably students from the nearby school, got off, followed by a man. Levy greeted him. They exchanged a few words, then climbed up the stairs, passing right by her. His eyes didn't meet hers. Not then. An employee ID card was hanging off the pants of the man who'd gotten off the bus. She waited a few minutes before following them inside. Then, without planning to, she bumped into them again at the cafeteria. She watched as they finished their coffee and walked over to the corner elevator. Her table was close enough to hear the bus man. "But Levy," he scolded, "I already explained it to you. I don't care what she told you or what you saw or didn't see. This story is finished, case closed. You've got to let it go." The man pursed his lips and adjusted the clip that fastened his yarmulke to his head. Then they took the elevator down to one of the subterranean floors—the employees-only corridors and the stacks.

. . . He regretted his actions as soon as he walked out of the library. There was no way back now. The security guard would remember him. They always greeted each other. The police would surely ask the guard if he'd seen anyone or heard anything, and if Johnny went back inside now, the guard would report that as well. Perhaps it might look like an accident, he thought, or a terrorist attack. In an instant, all of his ideologies and strong political views were gone. Yes, they'd surely think it was a terrorist attack. There were no shortage of Palestinian laborers and porters at the library, especially now, during the move. Johnny kept walking, never turning back. He took the stairs down to the bus stop and boarded the bus a minute later, leaving the library behind him . . .

She paused, created a line break between the short paragraphs, and added:

Johnny and Jacob, two archivists at the National Library, were clearing out the archives before moving the library to its new location. Down in the stacks, their years-long rivalry reached its boiling point, exploding with murderous violence.

Then she added, *Consider changing Jacob's name to Levy?* Then she deleted that last sentence.

She glanced at the clock on her computer screen and realized her time was up. She turned off her laptop, gathered her belongings, and rushed out to the bus stop. The conditions allowing her to write were limited. She'd felt that way ever since her son had been born—like she was living on borrowed time. Her own time, the time that belonged to her alone, was so limited that sometimes when strangers approached her on the street, asking for directions from here to there, or for some change, she was *this close* to yelling at them, *I've got a baby waiting for me at home, I barely have time to look at you!* It was as if the entire world was claiming time she didn't have to give. Sometimes the gestures she made in order to get it all done were so sharp and fast she thought her feet would leave the ground. But gravity kept her close to the floor. She made the 3:20 train, which meant she'd be home before Alex. That meant she'd be able to speak to the nanny herself, ask all necessary questions—did Lev cry, how much formula did he drink, did he poop, did he spit up a little or a lot, what did he play, did he do anything new for the first time? Alex always forgot to ask these questions, so when she came home after him she only received partial information and he felt as if he was constantly letting her down, regardless of what it was he'd forgotten.

As she descended the long escalator toward the underground platforms she felt satisfied with her day. For a moment, she let go of Levy's face, focusing instead on Jacob and Johnny, the two philosophy of science researchers and their confrontation in the dusty stacks. When the train emerged from the tunnel, she allowed herself to close her eyes. As always, ever since Lev was born, when she did this, his tender face appeared before her, smiling at her with endless sweetness.

Alex noticed the change in her right away. He was so glad she was writing again.

"I finally got unstuck," she whispered to him in bed, their legs interlaced. "I came up with a kind of character I've never had before." She said no more than that. She didn't have the kind of time she used to, to elaborate on all the different plots and characters populating her books and stories before they were even finished. Perhaps it wasn't about a lack of free time but about wanting to keep this new story to herself. At any rate, ever since their son was born, most of their conversations revolved around household logistics—who would be watching him when, what they were going to have for dinner, what their plans were for the next few days, when his next doctor appointment was. But there were still those brief moments in bed, when they whispered words of love to each other, making sure not to wake up Lev, who was asleep beside them in his bassinet. That day, Alex saw the change in her before she'd said a single word. As soon as he walked inside and she kissed his lips, he could tell that something in her face had loosened, the constant furrowing of her brows interrupted.

One Tuesday, she arrived very early, walking, as always, into the reading room that housed the library's collection on Judaism, the People of Israel, and Islam. She too always sat in the same part of the room, a quiet corner across from the Arabic scriptures. They soothed her, allowing her to work efficiently. Her knowledge of Arabic was so spare that the titles remained meaningless and inaccessible to her—the perfect writing environment.

She didn't see Levy, but the stack of books was set on his regular desk. The place was almost empty, and she allowed herself to take her chances and step closer to his desk. A small note was fastened to the stack of books with a paper clip. At the top was yesterday's date, and next to it the word *Levy* in handsome print. In spite of her curious urge to inspect the books in his pile, she did not linger at his desk.

* * *

A few more weeks went by, and all of her attempts to pick up the story where she'd left off were fruitless. Her Tuesdays comprised long hours of staring into space. Then, finally, one Tuesday, having struggled for hours against the document that refused to fill up with words, she got up to go to the bathroom and noticed Levy gathering his things. She quickly returned to her desk and packed up her belongings. Without waiting, she walked out toward the bus station. A bus was just pulling away as she arrived, and she knew it would be a few minutes before the next one came. She used the time to text the nanny as well as Alex, making sure she could stay in Jerusalem later than usual.

When Levy walked over to the bus stop she was sitting on the bench, covering her face with a scarf. The 68 bus pulled up and Levy got on. She did too. He took a seat in the front of the bus and she sat in the back. The bus moved toward the Central Bus Station. When it turned corners, she held tightly onto the back of the seat in front of her, to avoid getting slammed into the window or flying across the aisle. There were some boys and girls on board, chattering ceaselessly. She kept her eyes on him, and when she spotted him raising his hand to press the stop button, she tightened her scarf around her face and prepared to disembark.

The sun was in the center of the sky. The Jerusalem chill was already bone-deep even in early autumn. She wasn't used to this kind of cold. As she got off the bus, a shiver ran through her, and she regretted not wearing a thicker jacket. Levy paused by the bus stop, glancing at his cell phone. It was an old phone, the kind that didn't have a camera. A "kosher" phone. She stood behind the bus stop. A number 1 bus pulled up and Levy got on. She followed suit. When he turned around to smooth out his jacket, their eyes met for a split second, and she was filled with regret, but Levy didn't seem to linger on her. What the hell was she doing? Why was she following this man? What did he have to do with the story she was writing? And yet, four stops later, when he got off the bus at Shabbat Square, she did the same.

A woman was walking toward him, or rather a girl, wearing a headdress and a long, thin black dress. Isn't she cold? she wondered. The girl was pushing a stroller, the baby inside moving the way Lev did. They're the same age, she thought. Six months, maybe less. The girl's eyes were searching for someone, and when they hunted down Levy a delicate smile appeared on her face.

She shivered again. The baby was covered with a blanket, her legs twitching constantly, trying to shove the blanket off. When Levy approached, he bent down toward the stroller, and the baby greeted him with gurgling laughter, so sweet.

All of a sudden, she was horrified. How would she feel if someone followed *her* like that, interrupting these intimate moments with her son? For some reason it was obvious to her that this child was Levy's baby girl, and that the girl-woman was his partner. And yet she didn't budge, just stood there, watching them from a distance, no longer as careful as she'd been at first. The street was busy anyway.

Levy picked up the baby and held her up in the air. Her laughter rang out each time he raised her up or brought her face to his. The girl bent down to the stroller basket and pulled out an envelope that she tucked under her arm. Levy handed the baby to her mother and took the envelope from her. He rubbed the baby's head, and the group separated.

Levy headed on through the narrowing streets of the neighborhood, and she followed. He must have shoved the envelope into an inside pocket of his coat, because she could no longer see it. He walked for a few minutes more, then turned back onto the main road and entered a small shop. She kept her distance while he was inside. When he stepped out, she waited for him to move away before approaching the store window. It was an old-fashioned photography shop, the kind she remembered from her neighborhood growing up. As a kid, she would go into a shop like that with her parents to develop photographs from family trips. She recalled flipping through albums full of pictures from their Saturday hikes or visits to Grandma and Grandpa's, images which, to this very day, brought back nice memories of years gone by. She remembered how out of focus the pictures her parents took were, the frames never clean. Sometimes a finger had made its way into the image, blurring everything. Years later, many of her and her siblings' childhood memories were the ones documented in photos. If it hadn't been for those shots, they might not have remembered anything at all.

She found herself back at the train station. As often happened to her while driving, she had no recollection of how she'd gotten there. Her head was pounding. Perhaps she hadn't had enough water. She pulled out her bottle, but it was almost empty. She'd definitely boarded that first bus. How about the second one? She wasn't sure. She ran all the information at her disposal through her mind. She knew his name because she'd heard somebody use it, and there was that note on his pile of books, where the word *Levy* appeared in fine print, alongside a date. She'd also overheard that argument with the library employee, and then there was the rendezvous with the girl and the envelope. She tried to figure out if any of these events were connected. Did the argument have anything to do with the young girl and their baby? She was certain it was their baby. Two conflicting forces battled within her—one urged her to quickly process all of this information and try to find connections, explanations. The envelope. If she could only find out what was in it, she could solve it all. The second force pulled her back, away from there, away from Levy and his story. A voice inside of her argued, *It's none of your business. Who do you think you are? Who gave you the right to follow a stranger around?*

As soon as she walked through the door to her home, before she even went to see Lev, she ran over to the nursery and took her own temperature. No fever. That night, she insisted that Lev sleep in the bed with them. All night long, she kept hugging and kissing him, clinging to him and whispering words of love, though she knew she was risking waking him up.

The next morning, Lev woke up with a fever. It was the first time he'd gotten sick, and she blamed herself. She thought she might have given him the imagined fever she'd brought back from Jerusalem.

It was only the day after that, when the nanny called to report that she had caught the flu, and that she hoped Lev was fine, that she let go of her self-blame. Parenthood offered a constant sense of guilt she hadn't been familiar with before.

Lev's fever persisted for a week, going up and down, weakening him. They reported his condition to the doctor on a daily basis. She didn't sleep a wink at night, holding her ear to his little mouth, counting his breaths, resting her palm on his little belly to feel it rising and falling. One night, she was gripped with an awful anxiety. She woke up Alex and they took Lev to the emergency room.

The illness lasted for eight days, at the end of which

Lev woke up one morning, smiling, his fever gone as well as his flushed pallor. On Tuesday, she went to the library. She hadn't been there in two weeks, ever since that day when she'd followed Levy. On the train ride over, she realized the story she'd started writing wasn't going anywhere. The two archivists would be moved to her own private archive. Perhaps she'd just delete those opening lines and be done with it. Another failed attempt. She felt it had gone bad. The story had expired, and that was a sign. Stories weren't supposed to expire.

She didn't see Levy when she walked into the reading room, though his pile of books was there on his desk as usual. She walked over to her regular corner, but found it claimed. She returned to the central area and walked over to the row by the stairs. The desk next to Levy's was empty. She set down her things and bent over to look at his books. The note attached to them was printed with an old date. When she calculated, she realized it was the date of that Tuesday when she'd followed him, two weeks prior. He'd been gone from the library for two weeks, just like her.

Instead of sitting down and turning on her laptop, she walked over to the newspaper corner. Something unknown drew her over, she couldn't say what. *Hamodia*, a newspaper she'd never read before, was spread out on one of the desks, open to the back pages, where she saw the item: *The police are requesting the public's assistance* . . . And in the picture: Levy. Different, but definitely still him. Her heart pounded as she turned back to her desk. When she was in her seat again, she could feel it through the tips of her fingers, her pulse racing as if she were in the middle of a run. She pulled out her laptop, turned it on, and opened a new file. Then she typed as fast as she could, pushing away the guilt that had started climbing through her before the moment escaped her, before it expired. Her fingers clicked furiously.

She never thought literature could make a real, flesh-and-blood person disappear. And if literature could, she never imagined her own writing could have such a profound effect on a person's life, certainly not someone she'd never spoken a word to. But it happened. Not only did Levy vanish from the last desk in the row by the staircase at the National Library reading room, but he seemed to have vanished altogether, evaporating into thin air. And she was the only one who knew it was her fault. It was all because of that day she'd followed him through the city. She'd chased him away, she was sure of it, she was sure.

JUST ONE THING

BY ODED WOLKSTEIN

Central Bus Station

She felt her movement blocked before she even caught the murky glisten of the store window in the corner of her eye. She stopped short and quickly looked over the contents of the store. The attempt to attribute a kind of localized mercantile quality to the candy—lollypops donning dusty gilded crowns, chocolate bars whose faded wrappers poked through tasseled cardboard temples, and gift baskets whose lackluster gatherings were swaddled with shards of biblical passages about modesty and serenity—took away from what was left of their charm, blending them seamlessly into the atmosphere of the Central Bus Station: the odor of a closed office stabbed with news of a faraway fire, groveling with a lab culture of hominess, carried onward on the wind of scorched sweetness wafting from the bus platforms. She peered over the passageway leading to the food court, where the tired masses of the buses were deprived of maiming the road as they were bathed by the paleness of its lights, dividing themselves among its set compartments. The workers walked among the tables, rushing to remove the detritus of meals before diners even had a chance to put down their plastic forks. These workers alone, in the silence that wrinkled their faces, in the barren erosion paths marked through their layers of makeup, and in the restrained pomp with which their bodies rejected their uniforms, stood out in the sanitized space as the peeking remains of an old layer of soil.

She didn't need to spur the child on with words. In fact, she didn't even look at him. As she walked on, he continued to follow her, his arm held in her hand. She liked feeling the excess weight of his scatter-paced slowness—almost as if she were carrying him on her back. His steady, calculated resistance sent ripples of soothing tension up her shoulder. Sometimes she was pulled back, and then the sudden wakefulness of his gravity was as palpable as if he'd tipped over and fallen like an empty tent, but even then she needed to do nothing beyond slightly tighten her grip on his wrist. They were close to the plaza when the child paused again, this time emphasizing his action with a faltering stumble, veering in a decisive arch, then wildly overcorrecting, his mother's hand still gripping his forearm. She had trouble concealing her surprise: the gesture was too intense for this moment. Then she spoke to him, the words emerging raw and unprepared, their underdone texture leaving a greasy trail along her lips: "We're not going into that store before lunch!"

She was embarrassed by the real anger fizzing through her voice. When she let go of his arm, she noticed the ring of squeezing fingerprints quickly fading into the skin that had blistered as of late with a thin layer of tan roughness. She wrapped her arm around his shoulders and looked at him askance, as if to signal something wordlessly. The weight of shoulder blades dropping onto her supportive arm—not due to a loosening but rather a jigsaw of alert muscles—filled her with renewed confidence, and she gently led him through the foyer, occasionally maneuvering his path with amused shifts, lest he crash into the passengers emerging before them, floating like satiated fetuses on a heavy-flow estuary of dullness.

He walked ahead of her, flinging his limbs this way and that, as if feeding invisible birds, his heavy-lashed eyes frozen as a pair of foggy beads behind which glowed a spark of alertness. She often imagined these were his real eyes peeking behind the backs of their petrified guards. Unlike his cheeks, which bubbled up in an apple-like swell from the corners of his eyes, fertilizing the bottom of his nose with invasive flushness, his mouth was drawn shut, and only a close look revealed the trembling of sucked lips. His legs continued to drip from him like the final sputtering of a leaky faucet, but—as was the case whenever her eyes lingered on them—their movement seemed to be segmented, as if they repeatedly blocked their own sleepy momentum, turning this way and that as if in search of an escape route, the head wandering with them beneath the avalanche of mussed hair, smuggling its impressions through the hollow tunnel of his chest, until they accepted, if only barely, the conquered road ahead of them.

When they sat down to eat, the child renewed his protest, but it had none of that previous dizzy suddenness: the drumming of his feet under the table was joined by his stubborn silence and a kind of head shaking that sputtered from him whenever she parted her lips to address him.

"We'll go to the store after you finish eating, and we're only going to buy one thing." Then, after a brief pause, "You remember what the dentist said about candy."

By the time he responded—"Now, please"—his voice, and even more so his eyes, expressed an exhausted acceptance of the order of things. His grumbling popped like a bubble on the face of boredom.

She was about to answer him in a manner that would quell his game somewhat, when she noticed the man: standing near their table, tray in hand, eyes wandering this way and that. She noted the gray shirt stretched tight over his bulging gut, the signs of the tortured incarnation of a binge in the realm of newfound abstinence (an enormous pile of steamed vegetables flowed off the rim of the plate), the skin etched with stretch marks and the panicked gulping of air. She required no further proof.

"Sir, you're welcome to sit with us," she said. Her eyes fluttered briefly over the child's face, then returned to the man and didn't leave him until he sat down at their table with a sigh.

An acidic cloud gathered over them a moment later, so palpable that it seemed to dull the hubbub of the terminal.

The man nodded awkwardly at the child, and the mother moved the half-full beverage away from the boy's snaking hands in a near-imperceptible gesture.

The guest's pale face was anointed with an almost mossy film of sweat. Beneath his watery eyes, the nose camouflaged its moderate slopes with gasping cheeks, and the tongue reddened within the open mouth like a melting piece of taffy. "Visiting Jerusalem?" he asked, his hands sneaking over to the knife and fork beside his plate with a tentative caress—fingering and retreating and then taking hold.

"Enjoy your meal!" she said.

"I'll do my best. I'm on a diet."

She risked a slight show of interest.

"Diabetes. Recently diagnosed."

Relief shattered within her at once. To stifle its thundering crash, she shifted her eyes over to the child: he was now invested in his plate of food, as if pleading with it to form a ritual within a ritual. In her eyes, he was meticulous and perforated in every way, formed to the last of the shadow hatches in his chestnut hair: a work of art that had been completed before she'd had a chance to sign it. But she wasn't sure about this either: at times, her nose would scrunch up at the burning odor of fresh brushstrokes. It seemed he didn't grow up like other children did, with that sweet, sleepless languidness that everyone talked about, but overnight, with congenital flashes.

"Good on you for watching your diet."

"I do my best."

"It's our first time here—not mine, but his."

"Really?"

He seemed embarrassed to speak with his mouth full, so she elaborated on her response in order to spare him. "Yes. We've spent a lot of time up north. We love the green landscape, the water. But somehow we never took a trip to Jerusalem before, so we decided it was about time. Jerusalem is amazing. We won't have time to do everything there is to do, but at least I can give him a taste of the city. Show him what Jerusalem is about. I remember what it was like for me, the first time I came. Seeing Jerusalem for the first time."

"Very good. Where will you go?"

She noticed that the child ate slower the more he surrendered to the food. Under the table, his legs had stilled. She searched for his knees with her hands, but the gesture was too clumsy and obvious, and she gave it up. "I don't think we'll make it to the Wailing Wall, but there are so many other beautiful sights. There's Mount Scopus, the Old City, the Tower of David. We'll squeeze as much in as we can. As long as he gets a taste of Jerusalem. We'll get out of here and go where our feet take us."

"Very good." The man began lazily sorting his steamed vegetables—winnowing carrots from zucchini, mindlessly searching for pockets of flavor.

She noticed her son cradling his mouth as he chewed the remains of his food. In a moment, she would no longer be able to break through. She turned to their tablemate. "Sir—I don't even know your name . . ."

"Ameet."

"Ameet, nice to meet you. Oh, that's kind of funny . . . Can I ask you for a favor? I promised my son I'd buy him a treat at the store over there, and he's been nagging me about it ever since we sat down . . ." The confused look the man angled at the boy did not escape her. "Would you mind keeping an eye on our things while we pop over to the store? It would only be two minutes." She was already standing as the man pushed himself up against the table to let her through.

"Sure, no problem."

For a moment, she thought the boy wouldn't get up. When he did, it was as if he'd clumsily sloughed off his own self. With fast steps he moved away from his own image, which had been knitting dreamily into a meal that would never end while reciting some ancient spell with the labor of his shoulders.

"Just one thing!" she called after him.

He turned his head and looked at her as if he didn't recognize her. Then the spark lit up behind his eyes again, and she motioned with a heavy hand toward the candy store. He glided with careless blindness toward the chocolate bar shelf, and she caught his profile through the store window: his mouth was closed, but it seemed his entire face was torn in a joyous yawn, and she felt as if, after a long period of screechy instrument tuning, he'd finally found the right pitch. Her legs grew lighter and she sailed in his wake, stirring the smoky air as if mercifully making her way through a kindhearted crowd.

When she walked inside the store, the frozen lighting

glowed at her face, and for a moment she thought she was losing him. The white light was a falling rock and the candy was
shoved into its cracks like shards after an explosion. Then he
appeared again, a chocolate bar sparkling in his palm.

"Just one thing!" she said.

He looked up at her, slowly. For a moment, she imagined his head was satiated by the light—a white plastic spoon
bound to scoop up the entire store. Then he said, "All right,"
and she felt a tingling in her throat, and a sudden urge to shut
the window.

She looked this way and that, her eyes blocked by the
plaster-patched concrete angles, by pipes gathered with a
limp hand into a stilled air conditioner, by packages bare
of all name and image, shoved onto the top shelves, by wet
stains coming alive on the ceiling, turning its severe plains
into humps with the whisper of their expanding shadows.
She swallowed. She wished to say something, but the glass
wedged into her throat was now a floor, and something
within her flinched at the world which was flattened by its
transparence. She aimed her hand at the shelf before her and
closed her fingers around one of the snacks. Then she handed
it to him. "Here you go."

The child didn't take it, but she piled the candy at his
side, bending to pick one up whenever it fell, until finally she
gestured to him to put his hands together. The bowl of his
hands reflected in the glass floor that was wedged in her chest
but did not burden it, and she kept building her candy tower
until it almost reached the boy's chin. She thought she must
appear as a child lost in a hopeless game as she took such care
with a ritual that had become orphaned under his beady eyes.
She no longer saw the spark behind them, and imagined that
it had incarnated into the shallow glimmer of candy wrap-

pers, the cold halo of his stance, the light-fatigued floating of the glass prism against the billows of her trapped breath.

On their way back to the table, he carried the candy with both hands, and yet it still seemed to her that it would be lost from his grip, but that rather than fall, it would float over a city uninterested in its weight. A chill ran through her feet, and her eyes searched for stains and crumbs, as if wishing to fill her path with obstacles. But the floor tiles were brilliantly clean.

The two of them sat back down, and the child started eating his candy, one piece at a time, under the man's darkening gaze. She knew that, in a moment, the man would find an excuse to hurry away from their table, and that shortly thereafter they too would leave the Central Bus Station and, as they always did, get into the car that awaited them in the parking lot, and return to their home. She accepted it—after all, this was also the case on days when their little ritual was successful. And yet, it wasn't every time they did this that they encountered a confirmed diabetic. She gently pushed away the candy wrappers that had invaded their tablemate's territory—his name had already slipped her mind—and wondered if she'd manage to glean a handshake or a hesitant pat on the back from him before he left. She knew that even when he touched the child, nothing would happen to him. His figure would disappear among the tables without her being able to spot the weakness of his legs as they moved away, the slumping of his chilled shoulders, or the wild swaying that would attest to a dizzy spell.

Of course, she expected none of these. Apart from some sensational back-page newspaper articles, no sources claimed to document cases of hypoglycemia caused by touch. Besides, the boy was not toxic enough just yet. But now, as she wiped away a smudge of chocolate from her son's cheeks with apologetic stealth and flashed their guest a quiet, tired smile while he felt around for his belongings, it was easy to close her eyes and envision the moment when her son would conduct sugar like electricity, and circles on circles of diabetics would arrange themselves around him, devotedly extracting their bodies that were forced onto a prayer lost through eating customs. Beyond them, all around, she saw more and more pulsating and infectious circles, a thicket of spreading ripples, tens of thousands delivering the news out of Jerusalem as they leaned on their crutches or reached sleepy hands to feel for amputated limbs, until the glass floor collapsed with the weight of sweetness and the abyss gaping beneath it spoke her love with just-born lips.

ABOUT THE CONTRIBUTORS

YIFTACH ASHKENAZI is a writer and literary researcher born in Carmiel and living in the Jerusalem area with his wife Noa and thier daughter Tamara. His most recent book is the critically acclaimed best seller *Gehenna*, which is based on true events that took place in 2002 during his combat military service.

Avigail Uzi

ILANA BERNSTEIN is a writer, editor, and creative writing instructor. Her thirteenth book, *The Wrath of Tamuz*, was published in January 2022. She won the 2019 Sapir Prize for her novel *Tomorrow We'll Go to the Amusement Park*. Bernstein has taught at Bezalel College, the Hebrew University, and Shenkar College of Engineering, Design, and Art.

GULI DOLEV-HASHILONI is a writer for the film journal *Off Screen*, a master's student in global history in Berlin, and an activist. In 2021, he self-published his novel *From Worse to Worst*, written in collaboration with Emanuel Yitzchak Levi.

Silan Dallal

MAAYAN EITAN's debut novel, *Love*, was published in Israel in 2020; her English translation was published in the US in 2022 by Penguin Press and won the 2022 National Jewish Book Award for Hebrew Fiction in Translation. Her second novel, titled *The Scream*, was published in June 2023 in Israel.

Yanai Yechiel

LIAT ELKAYAM is a television and literary critic for *Haaretz*, and cultural studies professor at Sapir College. Her first book, *But the Night Is Still Young*, was a best seller that won the Ministry of Culture award for a debut and was translated into German. She is the recipient of the ADK's Berlin fellowship. During her time at the Sam Spiegel Film and Television School, she realized that the best thing about Jerusalem was the exit sign pointing toward Tel Aviv.

ZOHAR ELMAKIAS is a writer, translator, and researcher. Her debut book, *Terminal*, was published by Hakibbutz Hameuchad in 2020. She is the Hebrew translator of *Between the World and Me* by Ta-Nehisi Coates and *Going to Meet the Man* by James Baldwin (in collaboration with Yoav Rosen). These days, she is working on her doctoral dissertation in anthropology at Columbia University.

Oren Ziv

ILAN RUBIN FIELDS is a Jerusalem native living in exile. He is a film director and the principal of a Hebrew school. His debut documentary film, *The Prophet*, about the radical politician Rabbi Meir Kahane, came out in 2019. He is currently in the process of editing his second film.

Neta Levin

YARDENNE GREENSPAN is a writer and Hebrew translator born in Tel Aviv and based in New York. Her translations have been published by Restless Books, St. Martin's Press, Akashic Books, Syracuse University Press, New Vessel Press, Amazon Crossing, and Farrar, Straus & Giroux. Her translation of *The Memory Monster* by Yishai Sarid was a 2020 *New York Times* Notable Book. She has an MFA from Columbia University and is a regular contributor to *Ploughshares*.

Shai Davidai

TAFAT HACOHEN-BICK is a resident of Jerusalem and the mother of three daughters. She teaches literature at Ben-Gurion University and Achva Academic College. Hacohen-Bick is a postdoc at Ben-Gurion University's Center for the Study of Conversion and Inter-Religious Encounters, and studies literature and the climate crisis. Her poems have been published in literary journals and she is working on her first book.

Tamar Abadi

TEHILA HAKIMI is a writer, poet, Fulbright recipient, and winner of the 2018 Prime Minister's Prize for Hebrew Literary Works. Her book *Company* was published by Resling Press in 2018, and was preceded by the poetry book *We'll Work Tomorrow* (2014) and the graphic novel *In the Water* (2016), created in collaboration with the artist Liron Cohen. Her first novel, *Shooting in America*, is forthcoming from Ahuzat Bait. Hakimi is a trained mechanical engineer.

Avshalom Levi

NADAV LAPID is a film director, screenwriter, and literary writer. He was born in Tel Aviv and is currently based in Paris. His feature films have won some of the most prestigious awards for international cinema at the Cannes Film Festival, the Berlinale, and the Locarno Film Festival, as well as more than a hundred international awards. Theaters all over the world have featured his films, as well as numerous retrospectives of his work.

Reuben Castro

EMANUEL YITZCHAK LEVI is a poet (*The Sun Sings to Melchior*, Hava Lehaba Publishing, 2020), a playwright (*The Rite That Was Not*, 2018 Akko Festival of Alternative Israeli Theatre), and a musician (Emanuel and the Longings). He is also a master's student in religious studies at Hebrew University. In 2021, he self-published his novel *From Worse to Worst*, written in collaboration with Guli Dolev-Hashiloni.

Noa Eizenman Damron

ILAI ROWNER is a writer and translator. He has published two novels and a novella, and his last collection of stories, *The Player*, was published in 2022. He has translated Claude Simon's *L'herbe* in collaboration with Lilach Netanel. His last translation, of *Pelléas and Mélisande* by Maurice Maeterlinck, was published in 2021.

Jonathan Bloom

ASAF SCHURR is an Israeli editor, translator, and writer. He was born in Jerusalem in 1976 but no longer lives there.

Moti Kikayon

NANO SHABTAI was born in 1975 in Jerusalem. She has written and directed several plays and is the recipient of the Acum Award for a debut work for her book of poetry, *Iron Child*, which was published by Yediot Books in 2005. Her novel *The Book of Men* was published by Keter in 2016 and was one of five finalists for the Sapir Prize. Since 2015, Shabtai has been a theater critic for *Haaretz*.

Iris Nesher

YAARA SHEHORI is an Israeli novelist and poet. She was awarded the 2015 Prime Minister's Prize for Hebrew Literary Works, the 2011 Ministry of Culture Award, and the 2022 Agnon Prize for the Literary Arts. Her book *Aquarium* was recognized in 2017 with the Bernstein Prize for best original Hebrew-language novel and was translated into English by Todd Hasak-Lowy for FSG (2021). Her most recent novel, *The Age of Liars*, was published by Keter Books in 2022.

ODED WOLKSTEIN was born in 1970 in Ramat Gan. He is an editor and translator and is especially interested in the modern reincarnations of Gothic literature. He teaches literature at Sapir College. His third novel, *Rodent*, was published in 2022. He lives in Tel Aviv.